MATCHMAKING

the

Midwife

MATCHMAKING

the

Midwife

MADDIE EVANS

Philangelus Press
Boston, MA

Matchmaking the Midwife, Copyright © 2021, Maddie Evans.

ISBN: 978-1-942133-45-2
Cover art by Virginia McKevitt
Editing by Judy O'Gara

Matchmaking the Midwife is dedicated to all our healthcare workers. Thank you for your selfless service during an impossible year.

Chapter One

"Ella!"

Ella pivoted in the waiting room, heart racing. The practice's senior midwife stood near the desk with her hands on her hips and mischief in her eyes. "You get yourself into my office, lady!"

Ella shivered, mistrusting that jaunty look. Midwives knew how to seem confident in the midst of disaster, and Lori had just intercepted her between clients.

Had she missed a client's serious symptoms? Had she forgotten one of the practice's regulations? Was it about the delivery Ella attended last night?

Ella didn't even have the office door closed before the practice's senior midwife faced her with a broad smile. "Congratulations! Last night, you caught your fortieth baby— you're promoted!"

Ella's mouth opened. "Really?"

The silver-haired senior midwife hugged her. "The look on your face—I wish I had a camera."

Ella shook her head. "Well, Piper in the waiting room is probably thinking I got canned."

"Sorry. It's just this was the first time I've gotten a minute to talk to you all day, and in another thirty seconds, you'd have been with Piper." Lori opened her hands. "I've been reviewing your notes and documentation, and it's time. As of this late October afternoon, you—my no-longer-a-hatchling apprentice—are a fully-fledged midwife at the only birth center in Hartwell, Maine, with all the rights and privileges hereunto. Or whatever they say if there's some kind of ceremony."

Ella couldn't fight her smile. She could attend births on her own now. She could prescribe without having to run the scripts by another midwife.

Four years, and she'd actually made it. Ella struggled to collect herself. She had a patient waiting, after all. "I don't even know what to say."

Lori gave a roll of her eyes. "I know you. You're going to say, 'Lori, this is great and all, but I have a patient waiting.'" When Ella laughed, Lori shooed her out of the office. "Have you ever been to the taco place on Main Street?"

Ella shook her head. "Not even once."

Lori arched her eyebrows as she followed her to the waiting area. "Then I'm taking us all out to celebrate. Well, someday. Celebrating together assumes we're not all delivering babies at the same time."

Still smiling in the waiting area, Ella reached for her cell phone to text her husband the news...

...only to stop with her hand on the case, gut-punched.

Brett had died five years ago.

Even now—in an unguarded moment—Ella's immediate impulse after getting great news was to tell Brett about it.

Stupid jack-in-the-box grief. Reflex reactions, and the realization a heartbeat later.

Bracing herself, she called, "Piper, come on in," and led her into the exam room.

Piper got a look at Ella's face and froze before sitting on the bed. "What's wrong? Did Lori tell you there's something wrong with my baby?"

Terrific. Ella's first action as a full midwife was completely unprofessional.

"Everything's fine. Your baby's fine. I didn't mean to worry you." Ella forced a smile, but she could feel her mouth tremble. "Lori just promoted me from being a junior midwife, and I wanted to text my husband to let him know."

Piper was a nineteen-year-old first-time mom in her third trimester. She brightened up like a sunrise. "You can totally call him. I'll wait."

"See, that's the problem. I can't. He died five years ago." Ella tried to look calm and accepting. "It's not as if I'm still thinking about him all the time, but when I got the news, I thought, I have to tell Brett, and it caught me off guard." Steady breath. Click into the professional mindset. "So, Piper, let's talk about you and that baby you'll get to meet late November or early December."

The young woman clasped her hands between her knees. She was dressed in jeans and a stylish top that showed off her sweet baby belly. Ella, of course, wore what she considered the Maine uniform: a flannel shirt, workboots, and a lab coat with huge pockets. All the practice's midwives dressed that way. It worked for their job, the same way Piper's clothes worked for the job of being an energetic new mom ready to take on the world.

Ella's exam room fit right in with the flannel shirt and workboots mood, more of a bedroom than a sterile metal-and-tile office. The exam "table" was an extra-long twin-sized bed with a quilt, and alongside her wooden desk was a padded rocking chair for new moms to sit in if they wanted to talk. The windows all had flowery curtains. The whole birth center setup supported the belief that pregnancy could be the most normal thing in the world.

Piper threaded her fingers through one another. "Losing your husband must have been terrible. Is it one of those things you never get over?"

Ella gestured that Piper lie down, then palpated her abdomen to assess the baby's position. "You never get over something like that, but you do carry forward. Eventually, you don't think about it anymore—except when something wonderful happens, and suddenly you want to share it with them."

"I never thought of that." Piper frowned as Ella measured her belly with a tape measure, then snicked it back. Thirty-one weeks, 31 cm. Perfect. "My boyfriend is deployed. Navy. I worry about him a lot. Like, what if he never comes home?"

"I'm so sorry. You're measuring right on target, and I shouldn't have let my personal life worry you." Ella got out the doppler and the gel. "I have no right to share that with my patients."

"You're a human being. Isn't that like the first thing you said when I switched into your practice? That we're all human here?" Piper flinched as the cold gel hit her skin. "I'm sorry. This is only my second appointment with you, so this is way personal to ask. But five years—do you think you'll ever get married again?"

Ella felt for the baby's shoulder, then moved the doppler into the right place and turned it on. The whooshing sound of the heartbeat filled the room, and Piper closed her eyes as she smiled.

"Best sound in the world?" Ella prompted.

"Best sound in the world."

Ella watched the numbers. "And he's doing great."

"Cool." Piper sat up, and Ella got out the blood pressure cuff. "So really, would you ever get married again?"

"You can't beat perfection." Ella had realized after the first visit that talking to Piper was like trying to predict a game of pinball—you had to redirect her, or else she'd get a random idea and continue the conversation in that direction. Piper kept quiet while Ella got her blood pressure, and then before Piper could resume talking about Brett, Ella released the cuff and said, "This appointment is about you, not about me. Everything looks great for seven months, so talk to me. Tell me how you think things are going."

Piper's huge smile lifted the weight on Ella's heart. "He's

kicking so much! I love lying down at night and not falling asleep right away because that's when he wakes up, and I can feel him moving while I sing to him. He loves to put his foot right here." She rubbed the lower right side of her ribcage. "When he does that, I rub hard on his foot, and he pulls it back, then puts it up again."

Ella laughed. "He's playing with you!"

"Isn't that funny?" Piper beamed. "I wonder if I ever did that."

Ella said, "Is your mom telling you all sorts of fun things about her pregnancy with you?"

Piper rolled her eyes. "Are you kidding? I'll ask her, but getting an answer? Even getting a call back? My mother is the queen of the free birds. Never tied down to anything. I'm living with my dad, at least until my boyfriend and I can get married."

Ella said, "I'm sorry."

"That's just how my mother is. She didn't even tell my father I existed until I was like two years old." Piper laughed, not noticing Ella's flinch. "My mom's a bit flakey, but I've had so many awesome experiences, and now, when I needed help again, my dad took me in. He even gave me a job managing social media and doing office work for his business. He's the one who encouraged me to change from the obstetric practice because they were scaring me about getting an induction and an episiotomy, so he rocks."

Ella nodded. "It's good that you have an advocate in your corner. No woman should go through all this alone."

Piper blew out a breath. "I mean, my mom's *involved*. She keeps telling me I should name the baby Maverick, and that I need to wear him in a baby sling, and I need to breastfeed until he's five. It's just, she gets involved on her own time."

Ella tilted her head. "Did your mom have a hard time with your pregnancy?"

Piper pursed her lips. "As if. She's always on about how easy it was. Like, she told me to leave the other practice too, only she wanted me to give birth alone and not even come to see a midwife. That's what she did, so she thinks that's what I should do."

On a long, long list of things to do, doing "exactly what your mother did" wouldn't have made Ella's list. Especially something as dangerous as a first-time mom free-birthing with no prenatal care.

"Anyhow, now I've got you, too. A fully-ranked midwife." Piper beamed. "We just need to get you married off so you'll have someone in your corner." Ah, we were back to Brett, were we? "What are you looking for? Maybe a guy in his thirties, financially stable, smart, handsome, thoughtful?"

Ella winked at Piper. "Come to think of it, what I'm looking for is information about your pregnancy and how you're holding up."

Piper frowned. "You're boring. How do we catch up on nearly eight months?"

Ella checked her notes to hide her own uncertainty. How *do* you catch up on eight months when every one of those months would have been structured with guidelines about what to check, what to teach, what to monitor? It was a truism that "prenatal care" was something the pregnant woman did for herself in choosing her food, choosing her activities, and choosing her lifestyle. Lori had provided Ella a list of topics to cover at specific visits to guide the mother in caring for herself the best way possible, but Piper's surprise appearance in her seventh month had blown that schedule to pieces.

Lori had talked to Piper for five minutes before assigning her to Ella. "I want you to loosen up," Lori had added to Ella. "Regulations are useful, but human beings are messy."

No. Loosening up was for the pregnant mothers to do, not the midwives. Ella would just have to triage the impossible list of topics down to the most important. With a glance at Piper's chart, she said, "The biggest need right now is to do a home visit because you've chosen to deliver there rather than in the birth center. Normally, we'd do the home visit around the end of the sixth month or the beginning of the seventh."

Piper pursed her lips. "Could you come over tonight? Like at six-thirty?"

Tonight was Ella's free night. No on-call, no shift in the birth center. That could change on a dime, of course. If three women delivered simultaneously, no one was going to stand on ceremony about who should or should not be attending. But in theory, after five o'clock, Ella should be available.

What else did she have to do? No celebratory dinner with Brett. She would tell her mother the good news back in Connecticut, but that wouldn't take a whole night. Without anything else to do, Ella might have taken herself out to any of the restaurants in Hartwell, Maine—maybe that jazz bistro with the live music. In fact, she could do that anyway.

It would have been more fun going there with Brett, but in the past five years she'd done a lot of things without Brett. If Brett were here, he'd have wanted to celebrate her victory. He'd have wondered why she wasn't already trying out the jazz bistro, or the taco place, or the ice cream parlor on Main Street. Maybe Ella needed to return to doing those things.

Home visits took half an hour. By seven o'clock, Piper would want Ella out of the house so she could have her own meal.

Ella pulled out her phone. "Tonight's fine. I'll see you at six-thirty." Afterward, jazz. It was a date.

Chapter Two

As Adam pitched a load of garbage into the dumpster, his crew chief approached. "So, Boss, that couch—?"

Adam chuckled at the sparks in Ed's eyes. "You interested? It's yours. They were clear when they hired us to empty out the house. Landfill or your living room, it's all the same to them."

This was the kind of junk removal job Adam liked least but which paid best—and with a grandkid on the way, he wasn't turning down the money.

The story was too often the same: an elderly individual had lingered in a house he or she couldn't keep up with. They'd collected junk in their lives that they kept hauling with them from era to era, not asking whether it was still necessary. The junk and the undone tasks piled up, and no one from the family stepped in (or was allowed to step in) to take care of anything. There wasn't enough money, and there wasn't enough health. The person saved their garbage and buried their valuables. Eventually they died, and the overwhelmed heirs wanted everything gone so they could sell the house.

That's when they'd call the Junk Crew, and they'd trade money for cleanliness. "What do you want me to save?" Adam would ask, and inevitably they'd tell him, nothing. Clear it all, and they didn't care where it went.

Still, it was a bright afternoon in late October, and Adam would enjoy working in weather like this while it lasted.

Adam returned to packing stuff out of the kitchen. Most of Adam's crew were guys just out of high school, starting with nothing. After a month of working with him, they'd have their whole first apartment set up. Tables, couches, entertainment centers that no one wanted. They also figured out right quick the stuff nobody else would want: sets of china, mass-produced artwork, thousands of knickknacks. Adam had come to recognize the collectibles he might be able to sell. Most of them, though? Straight into the dumpster where they belonged.

The kitchen was done, so he opened a pantry closet that smelled of dust and stale breakfast cereal. He tugged the light cord and paused when he felt something heavy under his fingers.

Under the cheap bulb's faint illumination, he cradled the cord-pull in his palm because the cord-end wasn't a plastic doo-dad. It was a diamond ring.

He stripped off his work gloves and pulled out his pocket knife, then split the cord just above the ring. In the yellow light, he swiveled it in his fingertips to get a better look.

The ring was a wide band of gold around an oval diamond, with noodling down the sides and a row of tinier stones for decoration. Inside the band, it said, "Best Beloved, My Annette."

Wasn't this interesting? Even better, the client had told Adam to dispose of (or keep, or sell) the entire contents of the house.

Adam shoved the ring in his pocket.

Ed stepped in behind him. "Can you help me shove that sofa onto my truck?"

"Sure." Adam followed him out of the house, struggling to remember if the client had said his mother's name while discussing the cleanup job. Adam wasn't an appraiser, but that ring had to be worth a couple thousand. Maybe more.

A couple thousand bucks would make Piper's life a whole lot easier. Get that baby of hers a college fund set up right from the start. Everyone said the sooner you paid into it, the more likely the kid could pay for school. If Piper's kid went to college, he might not end up in a life like his mother or father had.

Or, for that matter, like his grandfather had. Not to say hauling junk was a bad deal. Adam wouldn't trade owning his own hauling company for anything. But you know, send his grandkid to college, and that would be a huge boost in life. Especially if the kid was as smart as Piper.

Ed faced him to lift the couch, but then stopped. "Something bugging you? Do I need to tell the guys to quit horsing around?"

"They're doing fine." Adam shook his head. "Just get this in the truck, and then I have to make a phone call."

Five minutes later, leaning against the quarter panel, Adam had the client on the phone. "We found something in the house you might want."

"I told you, I don't want any of it. Everything's too worn out, and there's mice."

Ed had flipped the couch over just to make sure he wasn't bringing home any rodents. Adam said, "In this case—"

"Unless it impacts the sale of the house, I don't want to know. Just get everything out."

Adam said, "Annette's engagement ring was hanging from the pantry light cord."

The client rewarded him by saying nothing.

Good. That got his attention. Adam said, "A ring like that, it's worth more than money, I think."

The client exclaimed, "Are you kidding me? Oval stone? Wide band? We looked everywhere. We thought the memory care unit stole it!"

The weight of it was burning through Adam's back pocket. "The same."

"It was actually her fiftieth anniversary gift. She never had an engagement ring." Silence. Then the man sputtered, "I don't want you to keep that. I need it back. I need you to drive it to me right now."

Of course he did. "I'll keep it safe. You can come get it when you settle up with me and we do the walkthrough."

The client drew breath as if to protest, then stopped.

Yeah, you think carefully before you order me around, sir. I didn't have to tell you about that ring at all. If I went by the exact paperwork you signed, you could have gone on forever thinking the nurses stole it, and my grandkid could have had a nice little start on his college fund, and it would have been totally legal.

The letter of the law was all well and good, but sometimes, you had to be human.

The client said, "That will be fine."

Good choice.

Adam glanced at the house. "I'll let you know if anything else happens, but we're on track to finish by the end of the day." Then he headed back inside because even with three grand of gold and diamonds in his pocket, he had a job to do.

Chapter Three

Ella parked her Subaru in the driveway alongside Piper's green VW Beetle—hardly the ideal choice for a Maine winter, and maybe something they ought to discuss. One of the items on tonight's checklist was the car seat, so she could bring it up then.

The bungalow was set back from a little-used road, with a creaky wooden porch, and a second story that didn't quite match the squared-off bottom floor. Ella mentally calculated how far they were from the nearest ambulance dispatch, and how far from the closest hospital. Not bad. If she needed to transport, they could have Piper in a hospital within a half-hour. More likely twenty in an emergency, and the hospital only required its on-call obstetricians to be within thirty minutes of the building. The doctor and the ambulance might arrive at the same time.

Piper met Ella at the door. "Come on in!"

The home smelled of onions and baking bread, and Ella reflexively took a deep breath. After the outside chill, a toasty house that smelled of home cooking was perfection. A tiny dog bounded up to her in the sparsely-furnished living room, tail wagging, while a dog large enough to pull a sled slowly raised its head from where it slumped across an entire couch.

Ella crouched to let the tiny dog sniff her hand. "Dinner smells awesome, but do you need to stay here and tend it?"

Piper chucked a dish towel onto the back of a chair. "Most of dinner's in the crock pot, keeping warm. Oh, so this guy is Moonie, and the big guy is Ricky. Here, let me show you everything!"

Not a problem. Ella would work fast through the entire checklist and get out in time for Piper to have her dinner.

Piper and the two dogs brought Ella upstairs, where a third dog met them on the landing, wide-eyed and just a little timid. Piper said, "I'm dying to show you the nursery! It's been so much fun putting it together. Oh, and this dog is Honey."

The nursery looked like the result of a baby shower registry stating, "Bring one thing from your attic," but somehow Piper had made it look adorable. There was a cat curled up in the crib, glaring at Ella with daring eyes as she reached over to touch a quilt. "Everything's so cute. Is this handmade?"

Piper picked up Moonie, and she giggled when the tiny dog licked her chin. "Maybe? I probably shouldn't let the baby use it if it is, right? Babies spit up on everything. How do you wash a handmade quilt?"

Ella measured the crib slats against her hand, then checked the drop sides. Cribs weren't supposed to even have drop sides any longer. "The crib isn't up to code."

"Really?" Piper pouted. "But it looks so nice."

Unfortunately, babies didn't sleep in the appearance. "The slats are too far apart. Who'd you get it from? Do you know how old it is?"

Piper shrugged. "See, that's the thing. My dad runs the Junk Crew, so all this stuff came from junk hauls."

Ella paused, wondering how to proceed.

Piper suffered no such uncertainty. "I know, I know, you're thinking, it's garbage because these folks wanted to throw it away, but Dad goes through everything and finds the usable stuff people are getting rid of because they don't have the room and can't be bothered to sell it. He's got a warehouse where he keeps the good finds, and there's a family shelter that's always calling when they need to set up someone in a new apartment. Either that or he sells it himself."

Ella nodded. "He repurposes the downsized stuff and trashes what's broken?"

Piper nodded. "For the last six months, he's been thinking about me every time he does a job, and if he finds something for the baby, he brings it home." Piper beamed as the dog licked her again. "I told you, he rocks."

Ella touched the quilt again. "That's why you don't know where this came from, or if it's handmade. Because it was left behind in someone's attic?"

"Yeah, but I spread it out in the sunlight and made sure there weren't bugs or mildew. Same with the curtains, the dresser, the rocking chair. Not the stuffed animals. I had to buy something for the kid, so I bought the plushy stuff."

It really was a "bring something random" baby shower, only all the gift-givers had no idea they were participating. "That's sweet."

Piper said, "I knew you'd like Dad," which set Ella back again because that wasn't what she'd said. Moonie wiggled in Piper's arms, so she set him back on the floor, and went on. "When you meet Dad, you'll be proud of how much he's looking out for me."

Ella said, "Will he be with you during the birth, too?"

Piper looked abruptly sad. "Yeah. They won't let Grayson come back for it, so Dad said he'd stay. But I think he's uncomfortable."

"I'm sure he knows the important thing is supporting you." Ella stepped away from the crib. "Which room do you want to use for the birth?"

All three dogs lifted their heads and ears. Piper hesitated as though listening to traffic on the road, then exclaimed, "Hey! Come downstairs."

Piper and dogs sprinted down the steps, Ella wondering whether Piper's retreat was supposed to be her answer. She could use any of the rooms, to be honest. Everything Ella had seen of this house other than the nursery was spartan. No knick-knacks, no generic artwork, no tiny hallway table with a display of ceramic birds.

As they reached the bottom of the stairs, the dogs rushed around the corner, and Piper called out, "Dad!"

Ella backed up while Piper hugged a tall man with dark eyes and a neat beard. He still had his jacket zipped. Then he looked over his daughter's head at Ella, and his brow furrowed. "Hey, there."

His voice was rich, deep like the brown of his eyes.

Piper grabbed his hand and turned to Ella. "This is Adam, my dad." She whipped back toward her father, more enthusiastic than a diehard Red Sox fan on opening night. "This is my midwife, Ella, that I told you about? She came to do the inspection so I can have a homebirth, and she's staying for dinner."

Ella exclaimed, "Wait, what?"

Adam said, "Home inspection?"

Piper dropped his hand and pranced into the kitchen. "I'll get dinner on the table, and you guys can talk!"

"Um, hang on." Ella raised her hands. "I'm just here to see where she wants to have the baby and make suggestions about maybe adjusting the furniture."

Adam had folded his arms. "And go through the house looking for safety infractions?"

"Like measuring the crib slats?" Ella forced a smile, but Adam didn't relax, and she shifted her folder in front of her chest. "I have to look at the car seat, too. The birth center provides a checklist."

His eyes narrowed. "Did we pass?"

"I haven't even seen the birth site, yet. She was too excited about showing off the nursery." Ella glanced at the kitchen, then handed him the clipboard. "Dinner isn't part of my visit. You can look at the list if you want to verify that."

He didn't take it as he unzipped his jacket. "That won't be necessary."

Ella added, "I was planning to check out the jazz bistro after leaving." Adam was still looking her up and down, and she fumbled for a way to mollify him. "You set up a nice nursery."

That was the first time Adam smiled, and Ella's heart caught. "Nah, Piper did all that. I save the baby stuff whenever I can, but she sorted through everything at the warehouse and got it in shape." It was comforting to see a man so proud of his daughter. "She did great with it, putting it all together. I wouldn't know the first thing about getting ready for a baby."

Ella looked around. "I wouldn't say that. The whole house is well set up."

He shrugged. "People abandon nice furniture all the time. It's a shame to chuck it out."

Piper returned from the kitchen. "Dinner's ready if you two will come in!"

Ella said, "Piper, I really didn't intend you to provide dinner. You said to come at six-thirty, but I figured—"

"You have to stay." Piper tugged Ella by the hand toward the kitchen. "I've only had two appointments with you, and you said it's important to get to know each other, so you're staying, and we're eating, and then you'll know me."

The largest dog padded in beside them, and Adam snorted a laugh as he followed. "You're in trouble. She does make up her mind."

Piper turned to Ella and winked, and suddenly it made sense.

Piper, the completely unsubtle matchmaker.

Ella glanced at Adam, unsure whether she should insist on leaving. Sure, Adam was tall and striking, but pairing up with the father of one of her clients wasn't something Ella had ever considered. He was younger than she'd expected, too. A woman Piper's age should have a father in his mid-forties, but he didn't look that much older than Ella.

"You sit," Piper chirped out, pointing to a seat, and then she and her father carried everything over to the table. A chicken stew, a salad, and yes, homemade bread.

With the meal laid out, Adam took a seat at the end of the table, and he fixed his eyes on Ella, suspicious. Well, why wouldn't he be? Ella sighed and braced herself for a home inspection during which she was the one getting inspected.

Chapter Four

Adam forced himself to look away from the midwife. Piper kept fiddling with her meal rather than digging in. He said, "You pulled out the stops tonight."

Piper feigned shock. "Oh, come on, Dad. We eat like this every night."

The midwife was doing everything to avoid his eyes. Seemed likely she was telling the truth, that Piper had sprung this dinner on her. Wasn't much of a mystery why. The midwife was skin and bones, and Piper had a heart for adopting strays. That girl must have figured her midwife was one good meal away from looking rosy and cheerful, and from now on, she'd end up bringing muffins or cookies to all her appointments.

Sneaking a look at Adam, Ella said, "It's all very good, thank you." She was kind of cute, especially with the way she darted her eyes aside rather than meet his glance, like a combination of shy and unnerved. She might be fun if she relaxed.

Ricky padded into the kitchen and sat at Piper's feet, hopeful. It wouldn't be long until Piper was slipping the mutt bits of chicken. Best to try getting the midwife talking if he wanted her to gear down. "Piper talked my ear off about your practice."

Ella brightened. "I'm glad to hear that. During her first visit, she was so upset by the way her other doctor had treated her." When Ella met Piper's eyes, Adam's breath caught. "I wanted you to be in a place where you felt listened to, and I'm so glad we were able to welcome you."

Piper had relaxed the moment Ella turned to her, as if that was all it took to dissolve her stress. After that last horrible medical practice…? Ella being so friendly was like being able to breathe again. Adam had suffered through too many nights of watching his daughter getting more and more overwrought as she prepared for her checkups, trying to figure out how to protect herself from the people she was hiring to help. "Find someone else," Adam would say, and then Piper would burst into tears. It was impossible, she'd insisted. She was trapped. She was trapped, and the doctor knew she was trapped. No one would take a new client so late in the pregnancy.

It turned out these midwives would. Not only wanted her, but also welcomed her.

Adam said, "Explain to me, what does a midwife do? Because Piper said it's just as safe as delivering in the hospital, and I don't see how that is."

Ella straightened her napkin on her lap. That woman was a poster for table manners. "I can show you my statistics, and you'll see Piper is right. In every category, we either match or beat the obstetric practices in the area."

Adam said, "Then why aren't you a doctor?"

Wide-eyed, Piper exclaimed, "Dad! You can't ask that!"

Ella shook her head. "Of course he can ask that! I love it when people ask that." She set down her silverware. "Obstetricians and midwives both deliver babies, but our philosophies are different. Think about if you went to see your primary care doctor about a headache. She might prescribe a painkiller, or she might prescribe a muscle relaxant, or she might refer you to a neurologist, right? If you went to an osteopath about a headache, the osteopath might check if your body was out of alignment and give you exercises to align the nerves and muscles. If you went to a nutritionist, the nutritionist might suggest supplements and increasing your hydration."

Adam frowned. "Okay...? But delivering a baby is delivering a baby."

Ella brightened right up. "An obstetrician is a surgeon, and a surgeon's mindset is to anticipate things that might go wrong. A midwife is a nurse, and we work more on the supportive side of things. The word 'midwife' means 'with woman.' That's our job, to go through the pregnancy and the birth with Piper as opposed to directing her. While obstetric care monitors for things to go wrong and then correct them, a midwife helps the process go right so we never get to the point where a surgeon is required."

Ella leaned forward as if she'd entirely forgotten to eat. Maybe that's why Piper thought she needed to feed the woman. "The two types of practices embody two complementary philosophies, and we're each working with a different set of clients. Ideally, our specialties can work together. Piper is a low-risk client, so expectant management works best for her. As long as we watch out for problems before they develop, she can have a hands-off delivery with a minimum of interventions. A woman with three chronic health conditions and a previous history of traumatic birth would be safest with an obstetrician in a hospital, continuous fetal monitoring, and the immediate option of an array of medical interventions."

Adam raised an eyebrow. "You're saying your stats are just as good for homebirth as a hospital birth because you give the difficult cases to the doctors."

Piper whined, "Oh my gosh, Dad..."

"That is exactly what I'm saying." Ella nodded with enthusiasm. "Women who don't require a high level of care will do better without unnecessary interventions, and my job is to figure out which women those are."

Adam raised his eyebrows. "But what if something totally unpredictable happens while she's giving birth?"

"Like what?"

Adam hesitated.

Ella pointed at him. "You've watched decades of Hollywood movies that make childbirth look like this scary scenario where the woman could explode at any moment. Can things happen? Absolutely. But are some of those scary things caused by the routine hospital interventions? Yes, so that's why we minimize those interventions. Meanwhile, I'm trained to handle emergencies that can pop up during birth. Cord around the baby's neck? Labor stalled? Baby stuck? We have techniques to address all those issues. Finally, we have the ultimate medical equipment: you live within twenty minutes of a hospital where our backup physicians have delivery privileges. I have a phone. I can and will call for help."

This was definitely the reason the midwife looked likely to slip down the drain. Dinner? What was that? Imagine if she talked through lunch every day at the clinic?

Ella said, "Of course we'll have medical interventions at the ready. I'll be monitoring the baby's heartbeat every fifteen minutes, and I'll be charting Piper's progress. We know all sorts of tricks to free a stuck baby. She's had tests to rule out high risk conditions. Plus, she has faith in her own body, and that means so much when a mom is choosing a practitioner."

Wasn't Ella just overwhelming? That made her a really good match for Piper. "I guess it does."

"Giving birth is hard." Ella's eyes were bright. "A woman who's giving birth should be able to put absolute trust in her caregivers and her birth partner."

Adam said, "So you've had a baby?"

Ella recoiled, and a momentary grief flashed in her eyes. What was that about?

Piper said, "You didn't get a chance, did you?"

"No, it never happened." Ella looked at Adam. "Five years ago, my husband died. We didn't have any children, yet."

"Oh. I'm sorry." Of course he'd have to say something clumsy right when their unwilling guest was finally enjoying herself. "You sounded like you knew so much about what women need during birth."

Piper said, "For goodness sakes, Dad, aren't you paying attention? She knows because it's her job."

Ella said, "It's all from books and listening to other moms."

Piper said, "And she got promoted today! She delivered enough babies that she's not a junior midwife anymore! That's why I wanted to celebrate."

Ella gave a nervous laugh. "I really just thought I'd just take myself out to the jazz bistro."

"Well, you're here. And I have dessert for us, too." Piper patted Ella's hand. "See? You don't have to celebrate alone."

Piper never stopped surprising Adam. Piper's first appearance had been a surprise, of course, when Kandace showed up at his parents' house one day with a toddler on her hip, a strung-out look in her eyes, and a request for child support. Not a court order, just a rambling story and a hand out for money. Ever since, then, Piper had surprised Adam in her reactions, in her spontaneous visits, in her equally-spontaneous animal adoptions, and in the kaleidoscope way she viewed the world. She had a lot of her mother's impulsiveness, unfortunately, but she also had a perception that Adam wouldn't have recognized as his own. Her heart went out to any abandoned thing, maybe because of how often her mother had abandoned her.

For as long as he'd known Piper, Adam's job had been providing a soft place for her to land. He'd gotten multiple court orders requiring visitation, requiring Kandace to tell him where she was living, requiring all sorts of things. He'd paid child support into Kandace's bank account every month for sixteen years and then into Piper's account every month after her eighteenth birthday.

Well, not now he didn't. Now he provided support in the form of a place to live and a job. Which wasn't entirely a surprise over the long term. The only surprise had been that when Piper was pregnant and unmarried, she'd come first to him. Piper might have an iron-clad bond with her mother, but she'd correctly identified the reliable parent.

Now here Piper was, providing care for her medical care provider. Again, a surprise.

Adam said, "You don't sound like a Mainer."

Ella looked aside. The passion was gone from her voice. "I'm from Connecticut. But after everything that happened, I went north."

Adam crinkled his eyes at her. "Oh. Not a real New Englander."

Piper looked about to crawl under the table, whereas Ella gave an exaggerated sigh. "Faux New England, all the way."

Adam said, "I can tell because real New Englanders don't use 'faux' to mean 'fake.'"

She cocked her head to the side. "You're closer to Canada, so you really shouldn't leave the Frenchisms to the stuck-up socialites on the incorrect side of the Blackstone Valley."

Adam spread his hands and shrugged. "You got me there. Why are you slumming, my ladyship?"

Ella laughed out loud, whereas Piper was likely sending mental signals to Ricky to rip out Adam's throat before he could talk again. This was getting fun.

"Is it okay if I just like Maine?" Ella said. "When it came time to move, I wanted wide open spaces and trees and snow."

Hartwell had all three in abundance. "Makes sense." Again, Adam wondered what had happened five years ago, how her husband had died, what had happened after. Why a woman who'd never had a baby felt called to deliver babies.

He drew breath to ask about her husband, but Piper kicked his ankle. Time for a safer subject, maybe? "Did you ever go skiing?"

Piper's plan to fatten up Ella, if that was indeed her plan, wasn't going to succeed. Not with one meal. Ella was quiet and proper and had the kind of self-conscious table manners that Adam didn't see from his junk crew. Those guys would just as soon pick up a potato and eat it like a hot dog if they were hungry—and usually they were. Heck, sometimes Adam would nuke a potato in the morning, wrap it in foil, and keep it in his jacket pocket. It warmed your hands, and then when you got hungry?—snack.

Yeah, not Ella. She had a precision about her manner of speaking. Total Connecticut gal, in that way. Her eyes crinkled when she smiled, though, and despite the French teasing, she didn't act like she was high and mighty. At the end of the meal, she brought her plate to the dishwasher, and she sure was a tiny thing. He could have carried her and a recliner out to his truck if this were a job, except she wasn't someone's discarded furniture.

Although, maybe she felt that way? Her husband had moved on. Not the same way Kandace had moved on. But still, it must have felt like her husband abandoned her by dying, and here she was, the leftovers. A couple of times Piper had grazed by the topic, and both times, Ella looked sad.

Five years, and she still missed the guy. How often was a woman that loyal? Kandace forgot Adam even existed until she needed something, and Adam wasn't even dead.

With the dishes in the dishwasher, and Piper looking like a cat with a canary about putting calories into her midwife, Piper said, "Let me show you where my baby will come into the world!"

She glided into the living room and gestured around like a *Price is Right* model showing off a brand new car.

Ella, who had spared a sentence before dinner to compliment the furniture, immediately said, "Could we move the recliner to have a bit more open space here?" Then she turned toward the woodstove. "It will be November or December when she delivers. Do you plan to use this for heat during the birth?"

Adam said, "Sometimes we do."

"Is it smokey? I'm concerned about the baby's lungs, but we do want the room warm. If the regular heater can keep it warm enough, I'd prefer that."

Goodbye, Ms. Crinkle-Eyes with a Shy Laugh. Hello, Ms. Safety Inspector, She Who Laughs at Nothing.

Ella paced the room, then turned to Piper. "I want you to buy three plastic shower curtains. We'll need those to line the couch and the carpet."

Adam said, "Shower curtains?"

Ella nodded. "Birth gets messy. Blood and water and sweat and tears. Also, at least two bottles of peroxide."

Adam glanced at Piper. "Maybe we should go for the birth center after all."

"Dad, come on. I really want this." Piper beamed. "Anyhow, Mom had me at home totally alone, so it's not a big deal."

Ella flinched. "That's a very big deal. So much could have gone wrong."

"She ended up at the ER later, but she said it was nothing." Piper shrugged. "But also, we have a hot tub in the back, and I wondered if maybe I could deliver in the tub."

First time Adam had heard about this. *How do you clean a hot tub after a birth?*

Ella only said, "I'm going to want to take a look at that."

For all Adam's reservations about the safety of Piper delivering at home, Ella seemed to have even more. After examining the hot tub, she paced from the couch to the front door, then checked the hallway to the garage. Then back to the front door. "This is the route we'd use for the EMTs if we had to call an ambulance," she said. "Also, if we need to transfer her ourselves, we need to review the most direct routes to both our birth center and the hospital."

No smiles, no crinkled eyes. Her precise movements and speech were even more streamlined, and she worked rapidly.

Adam tried a joking, "You were a junior midwife only yesterday."

"I've been a nurse ever since college. I only went into midwifery four years ago."

Adam said, "So, what else are you?"

Piper grumbled, "She's a human being who doesn't want you assessing her like she's an old upright piano."

"I worked at a nursing home right out of school, and after that I worked as a nurse at the elementary school." She glanced aside. "That's where I met my husband, but we never worked together. He was the principal of the high school."

Piper sighed. "That sounds so dreamy. My dad and mom never worked together."

Finally, Ella smiled, and Adam went warm inside. "Well, we never worked together, either. Not in the same building. That would have been dreamy."

Then it was back to the safety inspection. "I'm glad you have a new car seat. Those should never come used." Well, Adam just wouldn't tell Ella about the used one he'd set aside yesterday to install as the spare in his truck. "How does your car handle in the snow?"

Piper said, "Just fine. I take it easy."

Adam said, "I wouldn't let her drive it if it wasn't safe."

Ella looked up. "I never drove a Beetle, so I wanted to be sure."

Adam pointed to her paper. "Check it off. Carseat is safe. Car is safe. Move on."

As Piper darted into the kitchen, Ella double-checked the list she'd been marking up the whole night. "Okay, so you've got some homework to do, but not much. You'll need outlet covers and child-safe cabinet locks in the next six months. Get those shower curtains right away, though, to waterproof the couch and the carpet. Also, a new crib."

"I can get a new couch or a carpet every day of the week. I have a warehouse full of them." Then he hesitated. "Why a new crib?"

She looked up. "The one upstairs doesn't meet current safety standards. It's got drop sides, and the slats are too far apart."

Adam huffed. "I'm sure it's a perfectly fine crib."

"I'm sure it's a perfectly fine crib, too," Ella shot back, "but my job is to tell you it doesn't meet current safety guidelines."

He met her, eye to eye, and she didn't back down. Steely little thing.

She added, "Remember how we said my job is empowering women to make the best decisions? That means giving full information to make those decisions. Piper now has information. After that, I'm out."

Adam's nose wrinkled. "Are you saying you'd let her make unsafe decisions?"

Ella cocked her head. "It's not about *letting*. It's about respect, and yes."

This was such a weird interaction. Even knowing nothing about giving birth, Adam knew about doctors. "Can't you give doctors' orders?"

Ella stepped closer, and Adam tensed because for the twentieth time tonight, he'd been surprised. "Doctor's orders are for nurses to follow, not patients. Regardless, I'm not a doctor. I'm a nurse and a midwife, and my patients are in the driver's seat."

Adam said, "The driver's seat of a safe car."

She gave him a tolerant look. "I can give advice. I can facilitate. But in the end, Piper is the one providing ninety-five percent of her own prenatal care. I stand with her, and I support, but I do not decide."

Ella was so earnest, so sincere. Adam didn't want to look away from her eyes.

From the kitchen, Piper called, "Cake's ready!" and Ella started. She backed up a step.

Adam shrugged. "Well, then. Piper's decided it's time to celebrate your promotion. Seems you have no choice in the matter."

Ella snickered, and again to his surprise, Adam found he enjoyed making her laugh.

Chapter Five

At the door to her townhome's tiny deck, Ella silently watched a deer.

The creature had poked its head up at the very back of her yard, hidden so well among the thick brush that until she moved, Ella wasn't sure she was even there. Then she picked her way forward on reed-thin legs, nibbling a bush whose green hadn't yet yielded to autumn colors.

"It's going to be hard for you," Ella whispered. "Winter's coming, and the leaves will be gone."

On the other side of the glass, the doe kept browsing. Maybe it was for the best she didn't know what was to come. Being blindsided by pain was a different trauma than expecting it and preparing, only to have it slam into you just as hard.

Life had seasons. Even though the deer wouldn't understand, she was designed to survive this. Next spring and summer, this same deer would be thriving again, food surrounding her, without a thought for those frigid, lean months.

Outside was fall, but for Ella, perhaps it had turned to spring. Five years past tragedy, she'd changed her zip code, changed her profession, changed her outlook. Yesterday's grief had taken her by surprise precisely because of how dull the pain had become. How infrequent.

She still loved Brett. She always would. Until the day he died, he'd been nothing but good to her, but reality had its own designs. He stayed pinned in time while Ella moved forward.

The winter of grief had thawed. Maybe now her heart could step into spring. Those underground seeds and bulbs could grow again. The soil could warm. Snow would cede to rain, and life would return.

She shot three photos of the deer, the only way Ella had ever found it acceptable to shoot a wild animal. Then she checked the website for that jazz bistro. Could she visit it for lunch instead of dinner? Maybe her interest in getting out of the house was another sign of impending springtime.

Not real springtime. Sunrise came later every morning, and when Ella had stepped out of Piper's house last night, she'd been able to see her breath. For the rest of Maine, winter was just beginning. Still, Ella could cup her hands around that spark of warmth in her spirit and breathe on it to encourage growth.

The jazz bistro was, in fact, open today. Maybe she should check it out even though Piper had blocked her from doing it last night.

In retrospect, that had been wild. The house with all the pets, the hodgepodge of castoffs that fit together into a unified whole, and then that man walking in the house with the body of a weight lifter and the poise of a gymnast. Maybe when you hauled furniture for a living, you didn't just exercise muscles— you moved like you lived in them.

Then that mistrustful gaze, as though she'd manipulated Piper into coughing up an elaborate meal plus a whole evening's hospitality. The guy probably filled three dumpsters during the day and wanted to zone out in front of the television, only to find this medical interloper who required him to perform hosting duties.

Ella giggled as the deer continued to browse. Piper, with her transparent design for setting up her father with her midwife, was doomed to failure. Sure, Piper had talked Adam up to Ella with the enthusiasm of a social media influencer, but Adam wanted none of it. He didn't value advice from the not-a-doctor who dared criticize the spacing of the crib slats, and he wanted no interesting stories about Connecticut because it qualified as a New England state only on paper. He certainly didn't put trust in a midwife who hadn't yet peeled the protective plastic off her credentials.

He seemed fun, and he loved Piper, though, so that made him an excellent father. Adam might turn up for a prenatal visit toward the end, and he'd be there at the birth, but afterward he'd be just as glad never to see Ella again.

Ella's phone rang in her hand, and she answered in a soft voice, as though the deer might spook on the opposite side of the yard.

"Ella, I'm sorry to bother you. It's Piper's dad, Adam." Her breath caught, but he sounded too calm for it to be a medical emergency. "I was wondering if I could ask you a favor."

Adam walked down the driveway as Ella stepped out of her gleaming blue Subaru station wagon. Fancy car. He said, "Thank you for doing this. We can't get to work until the old woman settles down."

The Junk Crew truck was parked next to garage, and the Junk Crew guys were standing around doing nothing. Specifically, getting paid to do nothing.

Ella glanced toward the house where an angry woman had planted herself on a chair right in front of the door, arms folded, face pinched. "I'll try, but I'm still not sure I can talk her down. If her own daughter can't calm her, it's highly unlikely I can."

That's what Adam had thought too, for crying out loud. But no, running command control over at the warehouse, Piper had insisted Ella would talk sense to a woman who'd taken leave of her senses. Piper wouldn't back down: "Ella used to be a nurse with old people. She'll know what to do, plus it's her day off. I'll call her myself."

No, thanks. Adam was perfectly capable of calling for backup. What he couldn't do was bypass a resident who ranted that she'd fire a rusty shotgun at his guys, call the cops, summon wild dogs, and everything else she could think of. Ella was going to fail. No question.

"I don't think she's dangerous," Adam said. "Just disruptive."

"I'll try." Ella pulled a canvas bag from the car and slung it over her shoulder, then walked right up to the porch where that old woman sat with her eyes blazing.

Ella stopped at the base of the steps. The woman lurched to her feet and started yelling.

This again. Adam glanced at his guys, some of whom were already on their third cigarette. If they couldn't do the job today, he wasn't getting paid—but they still were. Ella had at max half an hour to get them in the building before he backed out of the job. Oh, and he'd also be good and done with the useless homeowner, who wanted her stuff hauled but didn't want to make the slightest effort toward making it happen.

How surprising, yet another out-of-control person wrecking everything, with all the reasonable people bending to their whims. Kandace wasn't the only one in the world like that.

From Adam's perspective, Ella seemed just to be letting the woman talk. Actually seemed like she was agreeing. Terrific. Adam had specifically asked her to get the woman to let them into the house, and instead Ella was going to end up convinced Adam was planning to steal everything. By the time this was over, Ella would be the one loading the rusty shotgun.

Five minutes. Ella was nodding still, but Adam noticed a change: the woman began nodding, too. She still looked angry, but then fear would come, and then finally vindication. The woman's stance relaxed. Ella walked up the porch stairs, and then the woman led her into the house.

As Ella followed her in, she waved at Adam: come in.

Not one to question a miracle, Adam brought his crew up to the porch. The owner appeared, wringing her hands. "I'll show you which rooms, but we'll have to avoid my mother's."

In they went. Most of what the homeowner wanted them to clear out was in the basement, so he sent his guys down to start hauling.

This job shouldn't have taken longer than a couple of hours. He'd already been an hour, and they'd only gotten started, but thanks to Ella they'd been able to start at all. All the tagged boxes came up from the basement, but the rest of the place was the definition of a hoarding situation. The homeowner had asked him to clear the entire screened-in porch, full of excess furniture and boxes, but now she hovered. Oh, should she really let that go? Shouldn't she try to fix that broken lamp? What if someone needed that artificial Christmas tree?

She was paying by the hour for her dithering. Even so, Adam showed her that most of the furniture wasn't usable. "Mice," he pointed out. Mice and heaven knew what else. Sometimes snakes. Definitely carpet beetle larvae. Mold covered the walls behind the furniture, and his guys reported the basement was full of the stuff. They were all wearing masks every time they went down.

He'd scavenge nothing from this site. He certainly wouldn't be replacing that beautiful crib with anything from this house, no matter how government-approved the slats. Everything ought to be burned, and then the ashes buried. He'd settle for dumping it.

As he worked, though, he kept remembering Ella engaging with that elderly woman. It looked as if she hadn't argued. She'd persuaded the woman without persuading, convinced her without contradicting, and then gone inside with her in peace. "Midwife means 'with woman,'" Ella had said, and today she'd done nothing to get Adam's crew admittance to the house other than to be with that woman.

Two hours later, Adam dispatched two guys with the truck over to the DPW to dump the load, and he settled up with the homeowner.

Ella escorted the elderly mother from her room. The woman had tears in her eyes. "You're leaving me with nothing."

"You have so much. See," Ella said. "They never touched your room. Your furniture in the living room is all here. Let's go in the kitchen. Can I make you some tea?"

The old woman kept bemoaning things that were gone, things that had been junk from the start but which she couldn't let go of.

The homeowner wrote a check, her hands unsteady. It wasn't just the mother who had the hoarding problem. Adam had seen much worse than this, and usually the issue wasn't only one person.

"We needed the extra space," the homeowner said, trying to absolve herself.

"You needed it," Ella said, returning from the kitchen. "And now you have it."

She left the house with Adam, looking over her shoulder. Her eyes were kind, her face distraught.

Trying to make her feel better, Adam said, "You did great."

"I only listened to her. She's so afraid." Ella bit her lip. "I'm glad I could help. The house is barely livable. They really should have gotten rid of more, but I guess it takes time. And courage."

Before Ella said it, courage had never seemed like a necessary component of cleaning up. But cleaning up required change, and maybe change needed bravery.

Adam pulled out his wallet and handed Ella three twenties. "I'm sure this is underpaying your nursing skills, but it's what I have."

Ella backed up and raised her hands. "I'm not taking money from you for this."

He shook his head. "I pay my crew. You gave up your

morning, and that makes you part of the crew."

She laughed. Adam was beginning to like the sound of her laughter, but she was nervous. "Please, no. I can't take your money."

"Suit yourself." He headed back to his SUV and pulled out his phone to text Piper. "You were right. Ella did it, but she won't let me pay her."

Piper texted, "!!! Go offer her dinner!"

Adam stopped in place. "Say what?"

"We stopped her from getting dinner out last night, right? Go offer her dinner instead of cash. Tell her you're making up for my mistake."

You are so just like your mother. Demanding, impulsive, quirky, and insistent on the things she wanted. Fortunately for Adam, there was no way Ella would accept dinner. He might—maybe— get her back into the house for Piper to feed her, but she'd never agree to going to dinner at that jazzy place with a guy like him.

Perfect solution. Ella would refuse, and Piper would have to find other ways of sneaking food into the woman. Plus, if Ella refused, Adam could do the honest thing and convince her to take the cash.

Adam caught up to Ella at her car door. "Since you won't let me pay you outright, what if I treat you to dinner?"

Eyes wide, Ella straightened.

He shifted his weight. How to convince her it was perfectly safe to turn him down? "Piper kept you from that jazz bistro last night, and you're acting like cash is an insult, so I'll give you dinner instead to even things up."

Flustered, Ella dropped her bag on the front seat. "You really don't have to."

"Yeah, I'm not feeling a gun at the back of my neck, so I must be offering because I want to." Well, other than Piper's badgering. He probably had four more texts from her already, insisting on having the conversation he was currently having. "Or you could just take the cash like I offered."

Ella's face swirled with emotions, intrigue as well as confusion, distrust, and enticement.

Hold the phone—what if she didn't take the money?

That might be interesting. Dinner and jazz and Ella. He hadn't taken a woman out for a while. Might even be fun.

Didn't matter. She was going to say no. A medical professional had no reason to take a meal with a guy who hauled garbage.

She shifted her weight and looked aside. "I'm on call tonight, so I have to be able to just walk out."

That wasn't a refusal. "When's your next night off?" She hadn't even finished saying Thursday before Adam said, "Done! Thursday, six-thirty? I'll pick you up."

Ella met his eyes and smiled. It left him hyper alert. "Thursday it is." She glanced away, then back at him again, shy. "And thank you."

Chapter Six

As Adam opened the door of his SUV for Ella to get in, she struggled to remember the ins and outs of dating. She leaned over to unlock the door on his side, but it was already unlocked, so that was a no-go.

Adam chuckled as he slid behind the driver's seat. "I got all four doors at the same time."

She bit her lip. "You're too trusting. Maybe I was trying to lock you out and take your car for a joyride."

He raised the keys in his hand. "Wouldn't work without these."

She sighed. "Hence why I abandoned the plan."

He turned to her with a big grin. "I didn't realize you had quite that sense of humor. You were so serious when Piper brought you home."

He had the most delicious voice. It was smooth like the way he moved doing anything at all. Even buckling his seat belt, he looked like a guy fully in control. "Being serious is my job. You didn't laugh while you were doing your job."

Adam paused. "Usually, we do laugh. A lot. It's not life and death with us."

He'd seemed grim clearing out the Bennett house, but Ella herself had gone grim when she'd witnessed the effect of decades of hoarding and anxiety. The mold alone left her wondering just how unhealthy that place was, and how two people had let it get so bad. They must have suspected, but they kept telling themselves if they couldn't see the damage, if they lived controlled lives in just certain areas of the house, then it couldn't be harming them.

All she said was, "It's not usually life and death dealing with pregnancy, either."

Adam shrugged. "Like you said, all I know is the movies. Delivering babies seems like doing security at a nuclear power plant, days of boredom followed by moments of panic."

"Fear, sure. Panic, no. But I guess there's never panic cleaning out a house."

Adam huffed. "There's absolutely panic, and no, I'm not giving you any details about that before you eat dinner."

The jazz bistro was just outside town, where Hartwell's roads transformed from orthogonal lines into a contorted maze that followed the curves of a very confused topography. Sedate piano music greeted them in the foyer, and they got seated in the dining area soon after. Before coming here, Ella had scanned the menu and made three choices about what she'd order, at three different price points. She'd wait to see what Adam ordered first.

Adam watched the piano player. "You ever play anything?"

She shook her head. "This place just sounded interesting. Once you get beyond high school orchestra, live music is fun."

Adam nodded. "I'm told the high school orchestra here is pretty darned impressive. They win awards and do musicals. Would now be the time to admit I don't know anything about jazz?"

Ella leaned back in her chair. "Then we know about the same."

The place had a nice feel to it, with low lighting, a stage area, that delightful piano, and a decent crowd. Diners kept their voices down, and the music wafted over everyone with a sense of comfort.

They ordered, Adam first and then Ella. Ella said, "I'm wondering how he plays for two hours straight."

Adam said, "I'm wondering how they got a grand piano through those doors," and that broke Ella up laughing. "No, really. The legs must come off. I've moved upright pianos, but never a grand piano."

Ella bit her lip. "Is that the weirdest large thing you've ever seen in a small room?"

"Nah. The worst are the triple dressers. Last year, we had one in a third-floor bedroom that weighed at least six hundred pounds, narrow bend in the staircase with a low ceiling to boot. We had to lower it out the window with ropes."

Ella said, "How'd it get in there in the first place?"

"My best guess?" Adam's eyes went mischievous. "They suspended it midair with a crane, and built the house around it."

Ella laughed. "Sounds like a job for a chainsaw."

"It was an antique, and the client wanted to sell it." Adam's voice pitched down. "Not everything we haul is garbage."

At the note in Adam's voice, Ella raised her hands. "I didn't mean it that way."

Adam side-eyed her. "We do move individual pieces sometimes."

"Just not grand pianos," she prompted.

He smiled. "Not yet, but looking at that one? I'd like to take a crack at it."

The food was good, and the background music made it exciting. Whenever Ella ran out of things to say, she'd watch the pianist at work until she either thought of a new topic or Adam introduced one.

Between songs, she said, "We're treading a line here because I can't really talk about Piper, since she's my patient."

"You can't talk about Piper, but I'm not bound by HIPAA." Adam chuckled. "She's a spitfire with a backbone of steel. She knows what she wants and doesn't think twice. She's her mother's daughter in all the wrong ways, but she's going to make it through. When that fellow gets back from deployment, they're getting married, and she'll be settled."

Marriage shouldn't be something you settle for, should it? Ella said, "She mentioned her mom is a bit flighty."

"Yeah, and Maine gets a bit chilly." Adam's eyes darkened. "I dated her mother for a few months back in high school. Summer ended, and she took off. Three years later she showed up at my parents' door with a toddler, saying, 'Hey, could you help out your granddaughter?'"

Ella recoiled. "Um, yikes?"

"I broke the landspeed record getting back to town. Piper looked just like me, so it wasn't a question, but we went through the whole dog and pony show. Paternity testing, child support order, shared parenting order. Three months after that's all set, I go to pick up Piper for my parenting time, and Kandace had lit out."

Ella bit her lip. "Could she do that?"

"Should she? No. Could she? She did. I'd get a court order, and she'd ignore it, and eventually I just stopped trying because nothing got enforced. My child support payments kept going through, and sometimes I'd get the kid for a visit, and sometimes not. Once I got Piper for three months because Kandace didn't pick her up at the end of my parenting time. Was her mom even still alive? Who knew? That was life until the kid was old enough that I gave her a cell phone so she could tell me where she was."

Ella shook her head. "I don't understand at all. Why wouldn't her mother want you involved?"

"Something's wrong with her. What can I say?" Adam shook his head. "I could always tell when Kandace hooked up with a new guy because suddenly she'd be interested in sending Piper again. Not sure whether she wanted to look like a dutiful mom or whether the other guy was mad that I was a deadbeat, but at least I got the kid for my parenting time."

Ella shook her head. "You're the opposite of a deadbeat."

"Kandace was the one spinning the yarn, not me." He glared over at the piano player. "Once I got a call that I should go pick up Piper from the airport because the plane would be landing in thirty minutes. Kandace had forgotten to tell me. But what could I do? You can't stop the payments. The kid needs to eat. Her mother was unglued, but Piper wasn't in danger, so I'd never have gotten full custody."

Ella sighed. "I'm sorry. How awful for all of you."

"Somehow Piper came out of that with a high school diploma and a wicked sharp personality." Adam drummed his fingers on the table. "Enough about my ex. How about yours?"

Ella flinched. "He's not really my ex."

Adam looked momentarily blindsided. "No, I shouldn't have said it that way. Brett? Tell me about him."

"He was a high school principal. Everyone loved him. They were building an addition to the high school. The construction crew had the school board and the administration there for a ceremony. I went, too, and—" She'd told this story so many times. "There was an accident onsite. It was entirely the builder's fault. I tried to help Brett. I couldn't."

Adam whistled low.

"They figured he'd never wake up He did, but he'd been without oxygen for too long." Ella bit her lip. "I took care of him. I did everything I could, hoping maybe we'd get a miracle. I took unpaid leave from my job to take care of him, and we had care teams coming in, as well."

She paused to get a grip. Adam gave her the space to finish.

"The insurance company went after the builder. The trouble was, as much as people loved my husband, they loved that other guy, too. He'd done work for just about everybody, so it all erupted. We were suing to get Brett's expenses covered. Then, when he died, the estate lawyer advised me to file a wrongful death suit. I was numb. I went along with it."

Adam said, "It turned into a firestorm?"

"Everything went inside out. People hated me or they loved me. I got glared at in grocery stores. People flung their trash on my front lawn. I didn't dare go out. I couldn't go back to my job because I didn't know what would happen. In the end, the lawyers came up with a dollar value for Brett's life, and I got the life insurance, and finally the dust settled, and everything was still wrong."

She looked back at the pianist. That might have been the "Moonlight Sonata," but she wasn't certain. Brett would have been able to identify it.

Adam said, "So you lit out of town and ended up in Maine?"

Ella shook her head. "They say not to make any large changes for a year after a spouse dies. On the one-year anniversary of his death, I sat down with a spreadsheet and worked out how long I could survive on the money I had, how much it would cost to get trained in a different discipline, what cost of living I could afford, and so on."

Adam looked vaguely shocked. Was Ella supposed to have just leaped from the frying pan with no planning? There were guidelines for a reason. Who knows what kind of mistake she'd have made otherwise? She continued, "With all the numbers in front of me, I decided to escape. I'd worked with the elderly, and I'd worked with children. It was time to work with babies. I could afford to take the training to become a midwife, do the internship, and work as a junior for a while. I thought to myself, where? We used to ski up here, so I searched for jobs in Maine, and Hartwell's clinic was hiring. I applied, and here I am."

Here I am was such a loaded statement. Here she was. Here, far from her family and friends. Here, unable to visit her husband's grave more than a few times a year. Or was she just here, in a jazz bistro listening to the "Moonlight Sonata" and eating dinner with a single guy whose daughter had picked out Ella as a potential girlfriend.

She met Adam's eyes, and he smiled when she did it. "Well,"

he said, "here you are. And I'm glad for it."

Chapter Seven

Adam eased up on the speed as he drove home because Piper would ambush him the second he stepped through the door, wanting to know how it went. Only he didn't know how to answer her.

He'd described Piper as surprising, but Ella wasn't exactly predictable, either. For one thing, she liked hearing about his job. Most women didn't. She caught on pretty quick to his nuances and his slang, and she wanted to hear the funny stories as well as the irritating stuff.

She got below the surface, too. When he griped about getting rid of still-sealed cartons from a move fifteen years ago, she said, "People do that all the time, even without the stuff. They carry everything forward when they should let it go."

She'd certainly let things go. She'd walked out of a whole life in Connecticut because she thought people hated her. Hated a widow for suing the irresponsible builder who killed her husband? Unreal. But again, people carried ideas around that they should chuck in the trash rather than leaving in their mental basement. Some old and friendly builder uses shoddy materials, and instead of everyone saying, "He scammed the school system, and kids could have died," they say, "Oh, but he always donated to the Oddfellows!"

It sounded an awful lot like, "You can't say that about your child's mother," when of course you should say the truth about the woman wrecking your child's life.

He slowed down to bump over the railroad tracks, then sped back up again.

Piper would want to know that he'd fed Ella, and Adam could answer honestly that he had. He'd even convinced her to get dessert, although she'd been too skittish for him to suggest they split something. Skittish, or distant? It was hard figuring her out. At times she'd say things that left him convinced she considered him beneath her, but then she'd say other things and it was clear she just wasn't conscious of talking that way. Connecticut was so close to New York City that you'd get plenty of spillover. It wasn't the same New England attitude he'd found in New Hampshire or Vermont, so maybe she just hadn't acclimated.

Piper jumped Adam the moment the door opened. "How'd it go? Why are you back so soon? Tell me! Did you kiss her?"

Adam barely got the door shut behind him before he parsed what she'd said. "Kiss her?"

"Did you kiss her? Tell me you at least held her hand!"

"It wasn't a date, Piper. Let me at least get off my coat, okay?"

Piper had the woodstove going, a small fire with the front doors spread and the grate up. It was more for ambiance than heat. When they wanted heat, those doors were shut and the pipe temperature topped three-fifty. Adam went to stand in front of it anyhow.

Wide-eyed, Piper followed him. "What do you mean it wasn't a date? You took her to a fancy restaurant where they played romantic music! You picked her up at her house. You should have stayed there and watched a movie and cuddled on her couch."

Adam relaxed in the easy warmth. "I fed her. That's what you wanted, isn't it?"

Piper threw her hands in the air. "Dad! I wanted you to date her!"

"You wanted what?" Adam turned. "No. She helped out at the jobsite, the way you suggested. She wouldn't take cash, so I took her to dinner."

"That's a date!" Piper pumped her head. "See? Dinner? Restaurant?"

"It's a one-off." Adam turned back to the stove. "We both had fun, but that was it."

She threw her hands in the air and stalked out, then stormed back in. "What did you talk about?"

Adam said, "We talked about you having a baby."

Her eyes flared. "You turned your romantic date into a ninety-minute medical consultation?"

Adam opened his hands. "What else would we talk about? We have nothing in common."

Piper started counting on her fingers. "You're both in your thirties. You both like your jobs. You both know me. You're both single."

Adam folded his arms and stared at her. The fire did feel nice. It was a shame about the fire in Piper's eyes. "We both speak English, and we both drive automobiles, too. You wanted me to put some calories into her because she's so skinny. I fed her."

"I brought her here to set her up with you." Piper ran a hand through her hair. "I can't believe you ruined everything. Text her back now and tell her you had a great time and ask her out again."

Adam raised his eyebrows.

"Do it! So help me." Piper put out her hand. "Give me your phone. She's going to be waiting for you to text her."

Adam said, "Back up a minute. Did she ask you to set me up with her?"

Piper spit out a laugh. "As if. She said she'd never get married again, so I wanted to surprise her by showing her how perfect you were."

Adam could cross "deceitful" off the list of Ella's attributes. That was something. "Then you're the one taking advantage of her."

"How? By feeding her dinner and then setting her up to get another dinner? She's the one who benefits." Piper folded her arms. "And if that place is as nice as the website says, she had *fancy* calories, to boot."

Not like in this house, where they cooked practical calories.

Piper picked up Moonie from the floor. "The point is, I'm going to get married and move away. That leaves you all alone, and right now she's alone, so if I put you two together, it works. She says she can't get married again because her husband was too perfect, but she'll get to know you and find out you're perfect, too."

Adam returned to facing the woodstove, watching the flames lick over the log behind the grate.

Ella didn't want to marry again because her last relationship had been so good. On the opposite side, Adam had seen how bad it could get. No reason to start anything else, no more than there would be reason to stick his hand into that fire and grab the wood.

Piper said, "Text her."

Adam replied, "Not now."

"And when?"

When? When Ella's first husband stopped being perfect? When Kandace stopped prancing through his memories because of her unstable choices? When Piper actually got married and moved away with her baby?

Piper's voice got sharper. "When, Dad?"

"Not now."

It was the only answer that made sense.

Chapter Eight

In between clients, Ella checked messages to find one from Piper. "I'm sorry to bother you, but I've been having a headache, and it's making me nervous that I'm getting that high blood pressure thing, so I was wondering if I could come in and get my blood pressure checked."

Ella's schedule was full today, but there was always time to fit in an emergency. With three minutes before her next client, she called back. "Piper, talk to me. What other symptoms are you having?"

Piper said, "I don't know. I might just have a cold and that's why I have a headache, but my throat isn't exactly sore."

"Blurred vision?" No. "Abdominal pain?" No, well, maybe, but not really. "Are you peeing okay?" Yeah, just fine. "Nausea?" Only when she thought about something being wrong with the baby. "Is he moving okay?" Yeah, just fine.

This was nothing. Maybe Piper had the start of a sinus infection, but Ella would give it 99% odds that everything was fine. "Why don't you drive over sometime when you feel up to it, and we'll put a blood pressure cuff on you? Don't worry about the baby. Lie down and let him kick you for a while. He'll reassure you he's doing great."

Ella explained how to do kick counts, since that would give Piper something to do as well as establish a baseline activity level for the final weeks of the pregnancy. Then she was off the phone and handling her next client.

Piper appeared in the waiting room at four o'clock, to all appearances healthy and unworried, with her father in tow. "I wanted him to drive me. In case something's wrong."

Something was definitely wrong, but it wasn't with Piper's blood pressure.

Adam looked worried, though, and that wasn't fair to him. Ella said, "Let's get you guys squared away so you can enjoy the rest of your afternoon," and brought them into the exam room.

Adam stopped short in the doorway. Ella said, "You expected metal and tile?"

"Well—" Adam looked at the rocking chair, the curtains, and the twin bed where Piper had immediately gone to sit. "Yes. Something sterile."

Ella said, "A doctor's office isn't sterile. It's just full of stuff that's white."

Adam laughed. "You have a point."

"Pregnancy isn't a disease." Ella wrapped the blood pressure cuff around Piper's arm. "How's your headache doing?"

"It's a bit better," Piper said, which Ella suspected was a lie inasmuch as Piper hadn't had a headache from the start.

"Is the baby kicking strong?"

"He's doing really good, although I think he tired himself out and fell asleep again."

Blood pressure was not only in the normal range, but in the low normal range. Ella charted it, then compared to the rest of Piper's records. The only times it had ever gone to the higher end of the normal range were her final two appointments with her previous provider, and given how she feared them, that might have been a case of "white coat syndrome."

Ella asked Adam, "Have you ever heard the heartbeat?" When

he shook his head, Ella had Piper lie down so she could palpate her abdomen. The baby shifted under Ella's fingers, and she grinned. Nothing was wrong, and Piper was entirely using this visit to advance her matchmaking scheme. "Okay, little guy. Time to show off for Grandpa."

Adam frowned. He was young to be a grandfather, but then again, he'd been a young father, too. Ella determined exactly where the baby's heart would be, gelled up that spot, and aimed her doppler.

A steady *whoosh-whoosh* filled the room. Ella listened while keeping her eyes on Adam's face, waiting for the second the huge grin overtook him, and he connected that he was hearing his grandson's heartbeat.

Oh, yeah. That moment. That was delight and awe and wonder. Suddenly, that baby was real.

Piper sighed. "I love hearing that."

Ella urged Adam, "Record it on your phone."

She let him get ten seconds, then turned it off. The baby's pulse had been steady throughout.

"I'm confident in saying your headache has nothing to do with the pregnancy." Ella handed Piper a paper towel to wipe the gel off her belly. "I suspect you'll be feeling fine in an hour or two, but if it's hanging around in the morning, call. If it gets worse, call immediately."

Adam said, "Thanks for checking her. I feel bad putting you out for nothing."

Ella pointed to a framed cross-stitch over the door, handmade by one of the other midwives. It said, "I would rather you call for nothing than not call when it's something." Adam burst out laughing. Yes, it was even embroidered with tiny flowers.

"Go spend the rest of your day gallivanting around town. Maybe visit the bakery and get a hot chocolate. Hot chocolate is great for babies."

Piper yanked down her shirt. "Could you maybe show Dad around the birth center like you did for me?"

Dear heaven, Piper was not letting this go. "I have another client right now."

"We'll wait." Piper looked at Adam. "Won't we?"

Adam said, "But you're delivering at home."

You had to credit the man for his common sense.

Piper folded her arms. "But I *might* be delivering here, so you should see all the facilities, that way you'll know how safe everything is."

Adam drew breath to object, and Piper hugged his arm. "Please, Dad? It'll make me feel better knowing you've seen how safe it is."

Ella glanced at the clock. "My next appointment should be done at 4:45 if you want to stick around."

Adam frowned. "That long?"

She nodded. "We like to spend time with our moms. It's easier to recognize when things go wrong if you've gotten to know them when things go right."

Ella was ready to be done with the day after her final client, but Lori stepped into the room and shut the door. "May I have a word with you about Piper Hurst? I was talking to her in the waiting room just now. She's really attached to you, and I'm concerned about what will happen if you're not on call to deliver her baby."

Ella shook her head. "It's even more complicated than that. Piper's trying to set me up with her father. She came in today for a blood pressure check due to a headache, but I haven't seen anyone fake a headache that badly since I worked in a middle school on final exam day."

Lori snickered. "That would explain why she turned down my offer to conduct the facilities tour."

Ella sighed.

Lori tilted her head. "You could just let her set him up with you. He's not a bad-looking guy, and his voice is melty."

"He's a great guy, but if he had any interest in me, he'd be, you know, interested." Ella shrugged. "Piper tricked us into having dinner together. He ended the evening thoroughly bored."

Lori shook her head. "Just don't marry him in the next two months. It's a conflict of interest if you deliver your own grandchild."

Ella's eyebrows shot up. "Duly noted."

Lori gestured to the door. "Go make our mom-client happy with a redundant tour, and then take off for the evening."

Ella had conducted the birth center tour dozens of times, but today her explanations felt stilted. This is a birthing suite. This is a hot tub. Here's where we keep the supplies. Here's a room full of used gear donated by previous clients for current clients. Here's the equipment we pull out in case of emergency. Here's an ultrasound machine. Here's the rear entrance where we can back an ambulance right up to the facility and wheel out a stretcher.

Following from room to room, Adam acknowledged the spectacular array of equipment whenever Piper prompted him to. The most he said unprompted was how neat everything was. The birthing suites were designed to look homey, with rocking chairs, soft lighting, and queen-sized beds.

In the hallway, Adam stopped before a wall of baby photos. "Are these all yours? I mean, babies you guys delivered here?"

Ella said, "Every one we have a photo for, yes. Sometimes parents don't want their baby's picture up."

Piper said, "We need to have ours up there. Maybe I'll take it. You can hold the baby, and Dad can get in it too."

Adam tensed. Had he caught on to Piper's machinations? Ella said, "Usually mom holds the baby while I take the photo, but I'll be sure to get your father in it."

Piper put her hands on her belly. "Hey, by the way—is this a contraction?"

Adam's eyes flared. "What?"

Ella rested a hand on Piper's abdomen. "That's a Braxton-Hicks contraction, and it's perfectly safe, just a dress rehearsal for the real thing. Completely nonproductive."

Adam sounded startled. "Why is she having contractions so soon? She's never had a baby before. How is she going to tell the difference?"

"Right now, you're feeling it here," Ella said, laying her hand toward the top of Piper's belly. "When it's showtime? You'll feel it there," and she placed her other hand on the small of Piper's back, then pressed both hands on either side of her hips. "When you feel that, I want you to call me, and we'll talk more."

Back in the waiting room, Piper said, "I feel bad keeping you late, so why don't you have dinner with us?"

From where she was folding towels on the other side of the waiting room, Lori rewarded Ella with a world-class smirk.

Ella said, "Answering your questions is part of my job, so that's not necessary."

Piper said, "It's no bother. We could go and grab pizza, or maybe that taco place?"

Adam was about to demure, when Lori called from across the room, "The taco place is awesome! Have you been, Ella?"

Ella turned toward her, wide-eyed. Lori knew perfectly well that Ella hadn't.

"You should try it," Lori added, finishing her throw-Ella-under-the-bus maneuver.

Piper rubbed her belly. "The baby definitely wants tacos."

Lori lifted the stack of towels. "Also, now would be a great time to review Piper's birth plan together, since her father is her birth support person."

Piper's eyes were huge, and she seemed so earnest. "Remember what you said before? That you have to see how things look when they're going right? Please come to dinner with me and my dad. You have to see how right things can be."

Chapter Nine

In his entire life, Adam had never raised his voice at his daughter. Right now, though, she was trying his patience.

Piper hadn't thought this through. In the restaurant, he could see right through Piper's transparent head: trying to figure out how she could ditch him and Ella so they could eat as a couple rather than as a threesome, only she wasn't having any luck. She'd already scanned the entire restaurant for anyone else she might know, that way she could join them instead. Adam might have been an absentee father—not by choice—but he'd spent enough time keeping up with Piper's devious spirit. Piper with her eyes this bright was Piper mid-plot.

Ella was sitting at Adam's side in the booth because Piper claimed she needed one whole side of the bench for her pregnant self, and he could see right through that, too.

Once again Ella did that thing where she waited for Adam to say what he'd order before she so much as breathed a hint of what she wanted, and her response after was so immediate that she'd obviously already chosen. Were both of them being crafty?

Piper kept looking around, but eventually she had to concede defeat: no one was coming to rescue her father from her presence, and therefore she decided to order dinner, too.

Ella teased her. "Are you afraid I'll critique your nutrition?"

Piper straightened. "You wouldn't do that!"

"At the twelve-week appointment, I usually review pregnancy nutrition. I'll spare you." Ella rested her chin on her folded hands. "Also, I'm glad to see your headache has eased up."

Piper gave a nervous smile. "Yeah. It's much better now."

The waitress got their orders, and Piper took off. "Sorry, baby's sitting on my bladder. Be right back!"

Smooth. Adam said, "I think I owe you an apology. I'm beginning to suspect she never had a headache."

Ella snorted. "You think?" She turned to him. "This is awkward, so I'll just say it. I believe she's trying to set me up with you."

Adam said, "She admitted it to me after I took you to the jazz bistro."

Ella didn't follow that up with anything. Uncomfortable, Adam added, "I told her to knock it off."

Ella glanced away. "Yeah, I figured you didn't want any part of that."

"Well, no, that's not what I mean. You're an amazing woman and fun to be around, but you don't need her meddling."

Ella puzzled at him. "Are you saying you did want her to set us up?"

Adam recoiled. "See, I didn't say that, either."

"I can't figure out your endgame." She traced her finger along the tabletop. "I was betting she would ditch us, though."

Adam said, "She's plotting an escape route. I assume she'll need to pee several times during this meal."

The waitress dropped off chips and salsa as well as their drinks. Adam took some, but then finally it had been too long since Ella last spoke, so he said, "Speaking of endgames, what's yours?"

Ella started to answer, then stopped again. Of course, if she could choose whatever she wanted, she'd want her husband back. Brett sounded like a good man, the kind of man she wouldn't want to forget.

Ella said, "I have a good time when I'm with you."

That wasn't exactly a vote of no-confidence. "Have you dated anyone since Brett?"

She forced a smile. "I tried twice, and it was nice going someplace and having someone to talk to, but there wasn't any spark. It wasn't fair to them. A man shouldn't stay in second place forever." She looked up. "Why'd you never get married? Because you had to take care of Piper?"

He shook his head. "In part. Given Kandace's instability, Piper needed me."

Ella let that rest. He added, "But Piper doesn't need me anymore."

Ella snickered. "She very much needs you right now."

"In a year she'll be married and living near some Air Force base. She's an adult raising a kid. I don't need to drop everything and buy her a closet full of clothes because her mother left her for three months. I do need to drop everything and answer her texts, but it's not the same kind of commitment."

Ella said, "You might have to babysit."

Adam prompted, "Also, now that she's grown, I wouldn't have to worry that her stepmother would resent her."

Ella said, "Fair enough. She's old enough to defend herself if her stepmother did."

Plus, Piper had picked Ella out for him, so she must have approved.

Piper returned. "Hey, chips and salsa!" She took a long sip of her soda. "What did Lori mean about a birth plan?"

Through the rest of the meal, Adam kept looking over at Ella and wondering what she was thinking. Was her hesitancy because of his job? Her spark-less dating experiences? Guilt?

A man shouldn't stay in second place forever. That was the sweetest thing Adam ever heard anybody say.

Kandace had lived her life as though the best anyone could

get was second place. She'd always be in first place in her life. Even her daughter took second place. Adam hadn't placed at all.

Even so, how do you steal first place from a flawless predecessor? Do you stomp in and break the world record, swinging for the back fence every time only to hear people criticize your record-breaking home run because the season's longer than it used to be? Do you wander the hallways of someone's mind, competing forever with a ghost?

The food at this place was reliable, predictable. So was Piper, who did in fact take two more leaves of absence to the ladies room so they'd have time to uncover their nascent romance.

Piper returned from her third bathroom break to say, "Can I have the keys and drive home? I'm super tired."

Adam said, "I'll just settle the check and take you."

She shook her head. "You and Ella should have dessert. I'll be fine to drive."

Ella pointed to the bench. "Sit."

Adam started at the take-charge tone in Ella's voice, but Piper immediately complied.

Ella's voice flattened into a school nurse's tone, brooking no nonsense. "We all know what you're doing, so you don't need to be sneaky. You want me and your father to spend time alone together, and you've spent the whole meal trying to come up with a plan on how to bug out of here."

Shameless, Piper nodded.

Adam sighed. "I don't have the energy to play games right now."

Piper held out her hand. "Then give me the car keys so I can drive home, and you can split a dessert."

That wasn't what Adam had been aiming for, but Ella said, "Deal. I'll drive him home after."

"Awesome!" She plucked up her coat and her purse, then looked at Adam. "I want a full report when you walk in the door, or so help me."

Ella watched her leave, grinning the whole time.

Adam rubbed his chin. "I didn't think you'd do that."

"I don't have the energy to play games, either." She shifted, and her thigh ended up alongside his. "Let's try this thing. We'll split dessert. We'll talk and see if there's a spark. I'll drive you back, and you can deliver a full report."

Adam didn't want to move, in case she realized they were in contact. "What should I tell her?"

Ella shrugged. "That's going to be up to you."

"Well, I could try telling her about this." Adam put his arm around Ella, and she leaned against him. It surprised him how warm that felt.

"Endorsed. You should tell her you hugged me." She rested her head against his shoulder. "Tell her you chose the dessert, too, because I have no idea what they sell here."

"They have five-thousand calorie fried ice cream extravaganzas doused in caramel syrup," Adam said. "She'll be glad of that. She thinks you're too skinny."

Ella said, "Then include that."

Adam wove his fingers through hers. It sent a jolt of energy up his arm.

Finally, he took a deep breath. "I hear what you said about a man not deserving to be always second place, but I'm never going to unseat Brett. He sounds like a stand-up kind of guy, and part of him became a part of you. You shouldn't lose a part of yourself."

Ella said, "It doesn't have to be a competition."

"You're the one who said second place. We all come around with the things we're carrying. I'm carrying Piper and the way she grew up. You're carrying Brett and the way you lost him." Adam squeezed her shoulder. "And the waitress is coming over, so in a minute, we'll be carrying a deep-fried ice cream ball with caramel syrup. Afterward, we can figure out what else we want to do."

A miracle happened: Ella relaxed.

With the question out in the open, she relaxed. Even without answers, she relaxed. She laughed at his jokes and met his eyes and smiled.

He found himself touching her. Touching her hand, putting his arm over her shoulder—just wanting her near. She did sit away from him on the bench so they could sort-of face one another while eating ice cream, but even then, she reached for his hand on the table. Her leg was near his, and he fought the urge to put his hand on her thigh.

It had been a while since he'd been out with a woman. Certainly not since Piper came home early this year, and probably not a while before that. He'd flirted, sure. Plenty of women wanted to spend time with a guy who owned his own place and had never been married, wasn't living on his mom's couch, and had no prison record. Standards weren't high when you were meeting people at a Superbowl party or helping organize the Memorial Day parade with the Oddfellows Club (where they called you once a year because you had two working legs).

With the tension gone, he found her electrifying. For one thing, she was wicked smart. She knew all these things about the world. If he mentioned some event, she could tell him the background. Was that the kind of thing that happened if you married a school principal? Or instead, was that the kind of thing that made a school principal want to marry a woman?

Not that Adam wanted to marry Ella. He wanted to have dessert and talk.

They left the restaurant in the dark. "Piper's going to yell at both of us if we just go back," Ella said. "Any ideas?"

It seemed like a waste to check out a movie. Plus, Ella was on call, so anything they did had to be something she could leave on a moment's notice. Adam said, "Town park. Let's see if they've got the winter lights up yet."

She walked at his side. "It's way too early for Christmas decorations."

"Yeah, those don't come for a while, but the town economic board started putting up lights a few years ago to attract attention. Soon as it gets dark early, they string lights on the path. You've never been?"

She shrugged. "I'm not very exciting."

The touch of her hand was exciting, but Adam didn't object.

The park wasn't far, so they walked until Ella breathed, "Oh."

At the park gate, lights glistened around both posts and over the archway. She stepped beneath it, then followed the trail of white from post to post. She pivoted, smiling like a child. "I never came this way after dark."

"This trail goes through the whole park," Adam said, "but not the whole thing is lit up."

She slipped her arm through his. "Let's walk as far as the lights go."

Their breath puffed up in clouds, and he wrapped his gloved fingers around hers. The path finally reached a pond, and they followed the path around it while the lights curled along a railing at the edge. They passed a family with a child plunking stones into the water, and then a man jogged by with his dog on a leash.

While they walked, Adam put his arm over Ella's shoulder. "This gets blocked when there's snow, but if you come here during the summertime, there's ducks. People have picnics."

The further they got from the park entrance, the fewer people they saw. Another jogger passed, this one wearing a headlamp and a vest with pink LED lights. "That's clever," Ella murmured as the pink figure continued around the bend. "I could use a headlamp when women want to birth in the dark." They were under the trees now, and although they could still follow the white lights, it was harder to see the gravel beneath their feet.

The trees parted, and they gazed up at the half moon, flanked by wispy clouds. Ella tightened her arm around him.

She sounded tentative, swallowed up by her winter coat, her cheeks pink with the chill. "Do you think we have enough to tell Piper?"

"Almost." Adam bent toward her. Ella stretched up, and her lips met his softly, sweetly.

He didn't want to let her go, but he did. "Now I can tell her that we kissed."

Chapter Ten

"Sorry, no dinner tonight," Ella texted while grabbing her homebirth kit and heading out the door on Saturday evening. She'd been dating Adam now for two weeks. "One of the dangers of the job."

Adam took it like a good sport. "Good luck. I'll see you tomorrow instead. Maybe lunch?"

Sunday morning, as Ella tucked a sweet-smelling newborn into bed at her mother's side, she got a second page to a second birth.

"Yeah, lunch isn't happening either," she texted.

Adam didn't sound miffed this time, either. "Did you get any sleep at all?"

She replied, "I'm a midwife. Sleep is always optional," and then she attended Sunday's birth.

Sometimes births stacked like this. You always prayed you didn't get four women delivering at the same time or you would have to call in your backups or do some serious juggling. In this case, Ella blamed the new moon. She blamed a storm front that came through. She blamed silly chance that two women with due dates two weeks apart would deliver one after the next.

Would deliver one after the next when she'd had weeks of solitary evenings when she could have delivered their babies, only now she had someone she wanted to see—and she couldn't.

During the births, she didn't think about Adam. She never dwelled on her own life during the long hours of labor because their birth wasn't about her. Adam said he contrasted his own life to his clients' lives when he was cleaning out their buildings, but Ella had no such luxury.

Births were time for meticulous charting, for listening, for awareness. She always had one eye on the clock because she needed to know: was the mother making progress? How long was too long? How far apart were those contractions? How long had it been since the membranes ruptured?

That all happened in one mental compartment. The other mental compartment was entirely empathy—and entirely focused on the birthing pair.

A baby was entering the world, and its entrance created a sacred space, something Lori called *the aura of the numinous* but which Ella always thought of as a pinch-point between earth and eternity. In that moment, one woman became a woman and a baby. A couple became parents. A stranger became family. If Ella had ever experienced the sacred, it was in those moments when one body opened up to reveal another body, and two who had become one became three.

"Welcome," Ella breathed as she guided the second baby into the open air while the mother gasped and the father shed tears. "Welcome to the world. We've been waiting to meet you."

There was sacrality in the new mother enfolding her baby into her arms, sacrality in covering the new person in warm blankets, sacrality in the parents gazing into the face of their child for the first time. Like an acolyte, Ella facilitated and channeled and observed, but otherwise she disappeared. In the moments when all went well, she allowed herself to feel awed.

Brett's death had verged on that sacrality, that "aura of the numinous," except with him it had been a fog of exhaustion and defeat. Babies emerged screaming, but Brett had winked out like a candle with no wick remaining.

There had been awe there too, but the kind of awe that led to "awful."

What, then, of Adam? Was there a smaller sense of the sacred in the meeting of two people who poised on the brink of mutual fascination?

She refused to think about Adam while taking care of the newborn. She performed the APGAR assessments at one minute and five minutes. She ensured the baby was warm and then helped clean up the mother. She weighed and measured the baby and did the baby's entire newborn exam while the parents watched. She made sure the baby latched on to breastfeed and verified that the mother wasn't bleeding too much.

For two hours, flying high on the cloud of endorphins being shed by the birth mother, Ella stayed on the peripheries while a family firmed up in front of her.

She wouldn't experience this herself, but she could assist others in getting a good start, and that was a blessing. Ella's loss could be these other families' gain. Without anyone waiting at home, Ella could take all the time necessary to sit with a laboring mom, coax a baby into the world, and then establish that baby in a safe place with confident parents who knew their own strength.

She'd give up a restaurant dinner for that. She'd give up a lunch date without a second thought, and not just because it was her job. But even so—it would have been nice to see Adam.

With the second baby settled, Ella slunk over to the birth center, bleary-eyed and counting backward to figure out what day it actually was.

Monday. Right? Monday. It must be Monday. She'd had four hours of sleep, and just about nothing was making sense anymore. Including why Adam's SUV was parked in the birth center parking lot.

Then he was getting out of that SUV and walking toward Ella.

Was Piper in there? Was she having problems? Had he called Lori and been told to bring her in for a checkup?

Except Adam looked unhurried as he crossed the lot with his coffee in his hand.

Ella rolled down her window. "Is something wrong?"

"Nah." He drawled it. "You look like you got dragged out of a ditch, and the last time you texted, you sounded strung-out." He handed the thermos of coffee to her. "I have a job this morning, but I thought maybe you could use some help."

She took the thermos from his hands, staring in wonder. "Thank you."

"Super high-test stuff in there." He shrugged. "I took a guess about milk and sugar."

"You didn't have to." She glanced aside, then back up at him. He was smiling. "That's really sweet."

"Well, I hope not too sweet." He glanced at the office door to hide his smirk at his own joke. "I'll quit bugging you now. You've likely got a long day ahead."

Before he could leave, Ella got out and gave him a hug. He felt so strong around her. So awake. He was limber and ready to take on the world, a full day ahead of him. He helped get her gear from the car, then walked her and her coffee to the office door.

From the waiting room window, she watched as he pulled out.

Goodbye. The word pained her. It hurt that Adam left, and that ache reminded her of Brett leaving her. It had been so long since she'd cared about being with someone. She was just so tired right now. Her emotions weren't following the right progression and had skipped thirty steps.

Behind her, Lori said, "That looks promising."

Ella didn't turn from the window even though Adam's truck was long gone. "Yeah, it does."

No, she decided a minute later as she dropped into her office chair. It didn't look *promising* because Adam wasn't promising her anything, nor was he asking for a promise. He was just showing up.

He'd thought about her. He'd heard about her back-to-back all-nighters and then considered what she'd need. Then, with no expectations, he'd done it. No promises. Just acceptance.

Ella closed her eyes and sipped coffee that was too sweet and not quite milky enough—but which was entirely perfect.

Piper hadn't stopped looking smug for days.

Adam didn't mind. Not entirely. Piper could saunter around the warehouse all afternoon looking as smug as she wanted. It would give her something to talk about with her boyfriend and maybe give the bum some incentive to tie the knot. A steamroller just like her mother, Piper would see her father happy and then turn up the heat on all four burners under Grayson's slacker behind. "You wouldn't want my *Dad* to get married before us, right?"

Maybe she'd go for the romance angle. "I hope my Dad proposes to Ella as a surprise. Wouldn't that be romantic? And they could get married right away because eloping is just the sweetest."

Adam had offered them a nice chunk of change to get it done. "You can spend it on a dress and a party if you like, but if you get the marriage license and go for it, you can keep the whole thing." Piper wasn't stupid. She'd love to have a big party, but she'd also love first and last month's rent plus security deposit. Adam couldn't afford to give her the down payment on a house. Not yet. Maybe if he'd kept that diamond ring, but you don't launch one marriage by destroying the memories of someone else's.

Kandace wouldn't chip in for a wedding or the rent, that was for sure. She'd wait until the day before the wedding and send some useless crystal bowl, and Piper would gush over it. Then she'd turn to her dad and ask if anyone had downsized a set of everyday dishware and cutlery.

Adam had started things off by getting a lawyer involved, putting Grayson on the hook for child support. Grayson would be on the birth certificate, and he'd have parenting time once the baby was old enough. He just wasn't...well, motivated. As long as Adam was taking care of Grayson's girlfriend and Grayson's baby, Grayson wasn't going to push too hard about marrying Piper and moving her full time into his life.

If Piper could leverage Adam and Ella to force Grayson across the finish line, all the better. Adam would have dated Lizzie Borden if it gave his grandson a more stable childhood than Piper'd had.

Piper poked her head into Adam's office. "When are you seeing her again?"

Adam huffed. "You're getting annoying about this."

She raised her phone. "A thousand people on social media need to know because they're sad you didn't get to see each other yesterday or Saturday. They also want pictures of the newborn babies."

Adam turned back to his computer. "You ever heard of privacy?"

"I'm not giving her last name, so it's fine. They all think it's totally romantic that you brought her coffee."

Adam rolled his eyes. "She was up all night. She'd be tired."

"That's why you're a catch. Everything else thinks it's romance, and you think it's Monday." She started typing into her phone, and Adam just knew she was taking a picture of him doing the accounting so she'd have a picture to post. He didn't follow her social media, but he'd seen a couple of times she'd prefaced a post with, "Photo for attention."

That was a thought, though. Adam reached for his phone.

At this morning's jobsite, he'd taken photos of before and after because he always did that for documentation. Nowadays, though, Piper had him and the crew chiefs "staging" the before and after shots so she could post them to social media. Ed had shot Adam's photo in front of the colorful junk ("before") and passed it along to her. Piper posted these pictures because she said it got people thinking about their own houses, what they could do if they cleaned the unused stuff out of the spare rooms. She also said people would like to see Adam's smile before they called, since it made him friendlier to have inside their houses. Dutifully, in all her photos, he was smiling.

He nabbed Ed's picture of him from their social media, then sent it to Ella. "Big job this morning." Then, after a few seconds' thought, he added, "Photo for attention."

If she had a client right now, she wouldn't be able to respond. But before he even set down the phone, Ella replied. "You look happy."

He texted, "Always happy to clean up a mess."

She sent, "With the size of that mess, you'll be working all night."

"We took that a few hours ago. I'm back now, and they're all clear." He followed that by sending the "after" photo.

She replied, "I stand corrected. I hadn't realized we were chronologically asynchronous."

Spoken like a nurse. He laughed. "I operate on a time delay. Speaking of which, why are you texting me? Aren't you at work?"

"Lori took my last client so I could go home and crash."

Adam typed, "Do you want me to bring dinner?" but then stopped because she didn't need that right now. "Chronologically asynchronous" also meant that while he still had a few hours left in his day, she didn't. What she needed was sleep.

He deleted that and sent, "I'll quit bugging you, then. Get some rest."

And then she replied, "Thank you so much for the coffee. It was really sweet."

Too much sugar? No, wait—she was repeating his joke back to him. Maybe she did think it was romantic.

He texted, "Good night, midwife. Dream sweet newborn baby dreams."

She replied, "And you dream about open spaces and empty shelves."

Piper was grinning from the door. "Well? Do I get to post an update now?"

"Get out of here. I have work to do." He turned his chair back to face the computer, but he was smiling.

Chapter Eleven

They managed to be at an Italian restaurant for lunch at the same time on the Wednesday after Piper's 36-week appointment.

"You can celebrate now," Ella said as she opened a menu. "As of today, Piper could deliver, and her baby would no longer be considered premature. We would not transfer her to a hospital, and she could have the birth she wanted."

Adam said, "Plus, the baby's smaller now, so it would be easier on her."

Ella paused mid-menu. "I wouldn't go that far. Her baby's right on track, size-wise, plus I think she'll deliver just fine no matter what the baby's size. A lot happens in the final weeks to loosen up her pelvis." She raised her hands as Adam looked up from the menu, bewildered. "I'm sorry, no shop talk. Just, it's not necessarily easier to deliver a smaller baby, and from a midwife's perspective, we love big babies."

Adam snickered. "As long as the father isn't the one being a big baby."

Ella choked on a laugh.

Adam looked abruptly concerned. "Does it ever happen that the birth partner passes out at the sight of blood?"

Ella raised both her eyebrows and her water glass. "If that's a frequent occurrence, please alert me now. Yes, it does happen. And no, I don't abandon the laboring mother to assist the birth partner. He or she can stay wherever they landed until the mom and baby are in a stable configuration."

Adam shrugged. "I've never done it, but I also never saw a baby born. Other than the movies."

Ella brightened. "And you didn't get the birth-partner talk we give at the four-month visit. Forget everything from the movies. Piper will not be lying on her back with her legs in the air. If she's in the hot tub, she'll be upright, and you'll see hardly any blood at all. I'll be lifting the baby from underwater, or she will, and after a while we'll get her out and wrap her in towels and blankets and move her inside the house where it'll be toasty." Ella paused. "There won't be constant screaming, either. She'll be making all the decisions she can, and I'll only intervene if she or the baby needs me to. Otherwise, this is her birth, and I'm there to be with her."

"You and your emergency equipment."

Ella nodded. "Of course. I'll be checking the heartbeat every fifteen minutes, and I can give emergency pitocin, or give the baby oxygen with an ambubag if necessary. My ideal would be never to be required at all, giving back rubs, suggesting position changes, and reassuring her. What are you ordering, by the way?"

Adam studied her. "Why do you do that?"

She froze. "Do what?"

"Make me choose first. Are you worried we'll order the same thing and the cook will die of boredom?"

Looking aside, she forced a laugh. "Yeah, when the lunch lady perished after making the nine thousandth slice of pizza, I took the weight of the world on my shoulders."

He didn't sound amused. "So what is it, then?"

She shook her head. "I'm... I was told that's what you do. You supposed to let the other person order first, and that tells you want you're expected to order."

Adam's brow furrowed. "Why doesn't it go both ways? Why don't you pick first so I know what I'm expected to order?"

Ella sat back. "I thought it was good manners."

"Well, today, I pick that you get to pick first. Then I'll color-coordinate my meal to yours or whatever standard you're using —" His eyebrows shot up. "Oh! It's a money thing. Well, I promise you, I'm not a doctor, but I'm good for anything on the menu here."

"That wasn't what I meant." Ella shrank back. "I know not to order off the top of the menu unless the host or hostess does, and don't order off the bottom if the host orders off the top because then you're implying the hosts are cheap."

Adam said, "Have you ever considered—and I know this is wild, but bear with me—simply ordering whatever you want to eat?"

The waitress arrived then, and Adam said, "She's ordering first," so Ella chose something off the middle of the menu. With any luck, that would be all right.

She hadn't meant to offend him. The whole rule about menu selection was designed to avoid giving offense, so how could that have backfired? Brett wouldn't have been offended.

For a while now, she'd kept comparing Adam to Brett. Adam carried an air of seriousness that made it hard to break through, but that meant he didn't try to laugh off Ella's own serious conversation.

Adam did make her laugh, though, and in the past five years, she hadn't laughed much. It was always a surprise, and always something that took her breath away afterward, as if she assumed that she didn't have the right.

The few times she'd tried to have coffee with a man, they'd laughed. Not the good kind of laugh, either. She'd mention Brett, and they'd laugh with a high-pitched tension Ella had come to recognize as someone desperate to avoid a topic.

She heard it from her clients at times. *How's your nutrition? Are you getting enough sleep? Have you and your husband discussed who you want there when you deliver?* They'd give exactly the same laugh and admit a package of chocolate made an excellent lunch, or that as soon as they announced that their mother-in-law wasn't welcome in the delivery room, they'd start World War III, so they were avoiding the topic.

Most men couldn't stand looking at Ella and seeing a woman who'd lost her heart and then carried on. Adam looked her in the face and asked to know more.

He'd gone through worse, in that nebulous way "worse" could exist when you tried to weigh degrees of suffering. For years, Adam had longed to provide for his child because that's what a man does: he provides for his child, protects his child, gets to know his child. It must have killed him when he couldn't.

Now he was doing all those things he couldn't do for years, being a steady influence and a rock-solid provider.

Adam was protective of Ella, too. Even when he'd needed Ella's help to deal with that anxious elderly woman, he'd tried to pay her. Why? Because for years, money had been his only way of providing for and protecting Piper.

Oh! Now that made sense. Ordering first was about the money. Adam thought she was criticizing his ability as a provider. He should have known the rule was there for a reason, so you didn't blow your partner's whole date budget on yourself.

After giving his order, Adam watched the waitress leave. "Now that the food's squared away, what's my job when Piper pops?"

"It's a job you're good at." Ella met his eyes. "Your job is to be her father."

He huffed. "I don't think I'm good at it at all. I was never around."

Ella cocked her head. "That wasn't your fault."

"It was my fault right at the start of things. I was eighteen and wasn't thinking very long-term, if you get my drift." He rolled his eyes. "I wanted better than that for Piper, but here she is, nineteen and having a baby with a guy who's ten thousand miles away." Adam's eyes darkened. "My father was different. He was always around. When I'd complain about him breathing down my neck, he'd tell me, 'Raise your child, spoil your grandchildren. Spoil your child, raise your grandchildren.' And he was right. I didn't raise my child, and now I'll be raising my grandchild."

Ella said, "Is it possible you rebelled when you were eighteen because that was your first taste of freedom?"

Adam huffed. "It's more possible I was eighteen and thinking with the wrong body part."

"Fair enough. But once you found out, you did everything you could for Piper."

"Did I?" He seemed haunted. "What if there was more? Should I have kept taking Kandace back to court to get her to abide by the ten court orders she was already ignoring? But I didn't want her in jail either because that would really mess up Piper."

Ella folded her hands. "Sometimes there's no good outcome. If it helps, I spent years second-guessing my decisions about whether to keep fighting for Brett's care even after the doctors gave up."

Adam frowned. "Why'd they give up?"

"Oxygen deprivation does horrible things to the brain. I kept insisting they try physical therapy, or new treatments, or new drugs. I combed the database of every clinical trial I could and made a case for several different experimental therapies." Ella shivered. "After the twelfth clinical trial refused, I gave up too. I cared for him until the day he died, but what if the next therapy would have worked?"

Adam said, "You got a picture of him?"

Ella opened her phone to the album of her favorite pictures of Brett. Brett giving a speech at his final high school graduation. Her and Brett at prom the year before he died. So many photos.

She hadn't paged through those pictures in a long time. Realizing that also ached in a way. Every year, the time rolled forward, and Brett stayed rooted in a past he could never leave.

Taking his time, Adam swiped through several. "He looks like a nice guy, but what happened to you?" He looked up at her, then back at the pictures. "You stopped eating when he died?"

Ella flinched. "Yeah. I guess."

"I don't mean that as a criticism. You look awesome, and back then you looked awesome too. Just different." He reached across the table. "I'm sorry if that sounded wrong. I happen to think you're gorgeous."

"Thanks." She squeezed his hand and then pulled back. "You ever look back at pictures of yourself when you were young, and in those photos, you look happy? Do you think of all the things you would tell that person now? Not that I'd tell myself not to get married. But I would have told myself not to take those days for granted. I'd have told myself not to blow him off on the days when I had too much to do. In the end, what matters is the people and the love you gave."

Adam murmured, "I can see that."

Ella said, "But there's not anything you could have told yourself back then. Piper's an awesome person, and if you warned yourself away from Kandace, the world would be a worse place without Piper in it."

Adam raised his eyebrows. "I can't talk to myself back then. But nowadays, when I see Piper making the same mistakes? I talk to her now." He sat back in the booth and folded his arms. "That's the only way I can change the past, is by changing her future."

Chapter Twelve

On a Saturday, Adam drove Ella to the county historical society. She'd enjoy something like that, and the greater Hartwell area wasn't exactly rife with museums. The only other museum-like thing he could think of was the Junk Crew warehouse and all the hauls in their various stages of processing.

That seemed *not* like something Ella would enjoy, so the historical society it was.

The weather had turned cold, and as they drove, she sat small in that huge coat. "I didn't know much about the area when I got here, but Lori gave me a book with all the history."

A couple of upscale gift shops sold a thin paperback with black and white photos and tiny captions, and it did a reasonable job of encapsulating three centuries of history. "I'm not sure what this place will even have. I've never been."

She smiled at him from the passenger side. "Well, if it's a bust, we don't have to stay long."

The Historical Society was in an 18th century Georgian house, and Adam's was literally the only car in the parking lot. An old woman roughly half his height answered the door. "You can look around, and if you need any help, let me know."

Thanks so much, folks—the next tour begins at two o'clock.

Adam and Ella found themselves in what perhaps used to be an old dining room, with a fourteen-foot-high embossed tin ceiling and two fire places, ringed with glass-covered cabinets, and filled with antique furniture that was roped off against anyone sitting on it.

"This is much more formal than I expected." Ella giggled. "Come on. Let's see what they've got."

In the cabinets, they encountered an assortment of objects, from a horseshoe to jewelry to an awl to a fountain pen. On other shelves, they found old photos, letters with crumbling envelopes, preserved wax seals, and a cameo with the image of Henrietta Hartwell, whose family used to own the dairy that served as the town's beginning. Spread out on one wall was an 1805 map of Hartwell.

"Amazing." Ella gasped as she approached it. "You can see the bones of the town laid out. There." She traced her finger a few inches away from the glass. "That's going to become Main Street. I think this is Farm Street. This one...?" She got closer to the map. "Overhill?"

Adam studied it. "That's Granite Cross Drive. Well, now it's Granite Cross. No idea when they changed the name."

"So much empty space. It's all built now." She cocked her head. "Okay, so where would your house be?"

He showed her where the brook intersected one of the main roads. "The railroad tracks come through here to avoid the hill, and then they curve back around so they miss the town center. I'm in the middle of the U."

"It didn't feel that far when I drove. None of the landmarks are there except the brook." She gestured to the lower left corner. "There's nothing where I live. Cranberry bogs or something."

Adam laughed. She added, "At least you get railroad tracks. Eventually. I just get townhomes and parking lots, and a bunch of wetland."

The next exhibit had a whole table to itself: "This piece of history remained locked in an attic in Guilford for two hundred fifty years: a cancelled check from 1858 with a two-cent stamp, from Mr. Leland Hartwell. When a gentleman found it in his Guilford attic, he thought it should come home to be enjoyed by the residents of Hartwell. The signature on the back matches the signature from the Town of Hartwell Annual Report in 1860."

Ella must have thought this was the most ridiculous exhibit she'd ever seen. Except then she surprised Adam by nodding. "That's history. Ordinary people making ordinary decisions, and for some reason, one moment of it gets saved and becomes so much more important."

Like Adam's rash decision on a date with Kandace. Like a builder's decision to ignore building code.

Next came the antique furniture. Which was junk, Adam realized—junk that had become valuable simply by outliving all the other junk. Maybe it had hidden in attics, or maybe it had been in everyday use until the historical society came around requesting donations. But two centuries ago, this was the kind of stuff Adam got paid to haul away.

Old chairs, a desk, a tiny table, a bed so fragile Adam would never have dared sleep on it alone, let alone with a companion. Adam imagined his 1792 counterpart, rolling up in a horse-drawn wagon and getting paid to haul this table and those two cabinets to the town dump.

The historical society had a china set plus a few tea pots and sugar bowls. In one cabinet was a find from an amateur metal detector: a metal clasp with three coins poised beneath it, everything in the position where it had been dug up, the fabric of the coin purse long since dissolved by time and the earth.

By contrast, Ella was gorgeous and alive in this setting. She read all the placards and told him the parts she found most exciting. None of it had seemed exciting, but the moment it became exciting to Ella, it felt more like history returned. "This bell came from the first schoolhouse in Hartwell! It was part of the schoolhouse in Juniper until it burnt down, and when the people in Juniper built a bigger school, they got a new bell and gave theirs to Hartwell."

Ella and history—it felt like a natural combination. Her history wasn't at all like his history with Kandace. Where Kandace had fled, Ella had stayed. Where Kandace had thought only of herself, Ella had thought only of Brett. While Kandace had sacrificed Piper's well-being in favor of her own whimsy, Ella had sacrificed everything for Brett's well-being.

What would Piper's life had been like with that kind of mother? Piper could have had stability. She'd have had two people she could rely on rather than just one. Or for many years, none.

"A cradle!" Ella exclaimed, crouching to get a closer look. The piece was dark wood and sat on rockers, with a hood over where the baby's head would be.

Adam said, "Don't look so excited. It doesn't meet current safety standards."

She looked up at him. "Really?"

He nodded. "The sides are dropped. You were so worried about the slats, but this one has no slats. Amazing anyone survived with those deathtrap cribs."

"Twelve to thirty percent of babies died in their first year back when these were being used." Ella stood and folded her arms. "Next question?"

Touchy there. He said, "At least they didn't have to worry about used car seats."

"Auto fatalities were much less likely in 1800 than measles, rubella, whooping cough, and the house burning down." She shook her head. "I know which world I'd prefer Piper to deliver in."

"Take it easy." Adam raised his hands. "I get it."

She side-eyed him, then moved on to the next item, a rocking chair. It would have collapsed under Adam, but Ella would have fit.

Oh, those photos of her and Brett. Adam fought nausea,

remembering the difference. He wouldn't have recognized her. Ella had lost at least thirty pounds after Brett's accident, and that off a frame where she'd already had nothing to lose. In restaurants, she wanted him to pick first to get permission to eat. When Brett stopped eating, had she waited and waited, only permission never came?

In those photos, she looked happy. Her broad smile had reached her eyes. Her face was relaxed, her expression easy.

Now, she looked drawn. Even when she smiled, she looked tense.

I wish I could make you happy, too.

She was young, still. He could marry her and give her a real home. Only thirty-five, she still had time to have a baby. They could be a family. She was a professional, and he owned a business. Menu shenanigans aside, he could provide for her. He could take her to music performances and area museums. He'd give her a home and warmth and meals, and someday she'd look at him with the same breathtaking happiness she'd had in those photos when she'd looked at Brett.

A man shouldn't have to compete for second place.

Could he make Ella that happy, though? Would she let him?

As they looked at an antique dresser, Ella slipped her hand in his. "This was a great choice. There's so much history here."

"Lots of the past." He glanced at her, but she was busy constructing a world out of bits of history. "Makes me think about where we're going in the future."

Chapter Thirteen

"Thirty-eight weeks, and thirty-eight centimeters over the belly!" Ella smiled as she retracted the tape measure. "Now, let's get a heartbeat on your little guy."

"He's moving like crazy!" Piper lay back on the bed with her eyes closed. "When I turn in at night, he thinks it's party time. Makes it hard to get to sleep."

"He wakes up once you stop moving because when you lie down, he's got a smidge more room." Ella palpated Piper's abdomen and found the baby right where he should be: head down, engaged, and facing her left side. She gelled up the spot over the heart and readied her doppler. "He's used to that schedule now, so for the first few days, he's going to have his days and nights mixed up."

Piper snickered. "Is that Mother Nature playing a joke on us?"

"The joke's always on us. Nature made them cute, so we'd forget the hassle and want to snuggle them." Ella applied the doppler, and a whooshing heartbeat filled the room. "He's doing great. So are you."

Ella got out the blood pressure equipment. "Mom called." Piper didn't sound pleased about that. "She sent me a baby blanket with 'Maverick' stitched across it even though I didn't say I'd use her name."

Ella inflated the cuff. "You can pick the stitches out of the blanket."

"I don't know. I mean, she's really pushing on that name. Maybe it's not too bad."

Ella said, "That's not much of an endorsement."

Whoa, that reading was high. Did Ella take it right? Steadying her voice, Ella said, "Blood pressure's a bit on the high side. Why don't you lie down on your left side, and we'll get that again in a few minutes."

Piper sighed. "It would figure. I won't be able to birth at home now, either."

"The reading may have been wrong. I can use a different cuff." Or maybe Piper was unbelievably upset, and it would do to calm her a bit. Ella pulled out her folder. "We've talked about birth plans before, and how you can't really plan a birth, but why don't we spend the next five minutes going over your preferences again. I know you want the tub. And you want the dogs there, right? And all my moms say that first cup of coffee after they give birth…? It's the best they've ever had."

Piper closed her eyes. "That might be good."

Ella prompted, "I bet your dad would make you the world's tastiest breakfast sandwich if you asked. Bacon, egg, cheddar, a toasted bulkie roll…?"

Piper smiled. "I read a story where after the delivery, everybody sang 'Happy Birthday to You' to the baby. Can we do that?"

"That sounds like a lovely plan." Piper was already relaxing. Five minutes of this and she'd be fine. "What else do you think would be nice?"

Piper's mouth twitched. "Well, I already can't have Grayson here, so there goes my number one preference."

"I'm sorry, honey." Ella shook her head. "It's a shame, but we'll get him video and pictures as soon as possible."

"I miss him." Piper bit her lip. "We didn't have enough time together. We were dating, and then I got pregnant, and then he went overseas. Once I find out when he's coming back, I'll have to throw together the wedding real quick, but it's hard to wait."

Ella sat back. "If you haven't spent that much time together, what's the rush?"

Piper pointed to her abdomen.

Ella shook her head. "A baby doesn't make a new relationship easier. If anything, it's going to make things harder to have a baby in between you."

Piper raised her head. "It's not like we have a choice."

"Of course you have a choice, and keep your head down." When Piper was flat again, Ella said, "Since you've got the legal stuff settled, why not wait a year? Get married on your baby's first birthday. Grayson's going to come back a different person after deployment, so give him a chance to get settled back into his life. Let him get to know himself again. You're going to be a different person too, once you're a mom. You'll also need to get to know who you are again."

Piper picked up her head again. "That makes it more important to get married. What if he changes and I change, and then we're not right for each other anymore?"

Ella pointed to the pillow, and Piper went back down. "You're going to have a better chance at things if you're not getting to know yourself all over again, getting to know him all over again, as well as getting to know a brand-new person."

Piper's nose wrinkled. "You think so?"

Ella said, "They tell you not to make too many big changes all at once."

Piper frowned. "After Brent died, you moved and started a new career."

"I stayed put for a year, just like the books said. I continued my nursing career, and then I started taking the classes I'd need to switch specialties." Ella nodded. "When you jump from one thing into another too fast, sometimes you're doing it because you're afraid of being left with nothing."

Piper said, "You *were* left with nothing."

Ella said, "So look at me, and trust that a bad 'something' is worse than nothing."

Piper said, "But you're dating my dad, so you didn't want to be left with nothing, either."

Ella had been seeing Adam now for about five weeks. It was definitely not "nothing." He was thoughtful and strong, and he was a good listener. She'd forgotten the comfort of knowing a man was present on the other end of the phone, ready to text her something strange he'd found during a cleanup. Over the weeks, she'd begun picking up his vocabulary for his work and begun knowing the kinds of things he looked for when assessing a job. She admired the way he separated out some of the better furniture and donated it to a family shelter rather than selling it. She'd come to appreciate the pride he took in walking into a mess someone else had created and walking out again with everything organized at his back.

Ella said, "I'm not saying to choose nothing over Grayson. What I'm saying is that since you don't want to lose Grayson, waiting might give you a better chance of keeping him."

Piper said, "He does love me."

Ella raised her hands. "His love for you is not in question. What's in question is your communication, your ability to negotiate, your sense of what to compromise and when to compromise it, and what's for the best for all three of you over the long term."

Piper stayed silent.

Ella said, "When you marry him, you should be sure you're choosing him, not resorting to him. He deserves to be your first choice."

Piper frowned. "I see what you mean." Then she looked up. "Dad says it's best for the baby if we get married as soon as we can."

Ella said, "Your father has a point, but don't you think what's best for your baby is having parents who are in a good place emotionally? Your baby needs parents who can form a strong bond with one another. Your father's not wrong about the what, but you might want to think twice about the when. And speaking of time, let's get your blood pressure again."

Ella inflated the cuff. "Think of all the things you could do with an extra year to plan your wedding. Your baby might even be walking by then. You could put him in a tiny tuxedo and make him your ring bearer."

Piper grinned. The cuff released, and Ella smiled. Much better blood pressure this time. "You're fine. We'll get this once more before you leave, just to be sure, but I bet that first reading was an outlier."

Piper sat up, but rather than looking confident, instead she wove her fingers together and put her hands between her knees. "If we don't get married right away... I don't want to be a disappointment to Dad."

"Honey, you're never going to be a disappointment to your father." Ella rested a hand on Piper's shoulder. How many times had she had conversations like this with students at school? Kids who were sick over their grades, kids who were depressed and afraid to tell their parents because their parents would be disappointed—when actually, their parents would be more upset to know their children were shouldering that entire burden themselves. "Your father loves you and wants what's best for you. He wants you to be happy. He'd be more disappointed if you made yourself unhappy to please him."

Piper swallowed hard as Ella returned to her chair. "I want everything to work out. I want Grayson to come home. I want to be a family with our baby."

"Then that's what you want." Ella sat back. "But do it because you want it, not because anyone else expects it."

Chapter Fourteen

Piper bounded back into the Junk Crew office with a huge smile. "Ella says the baby's doing great!" she sing-songed so it echoed from all the walls. "Also, we told the baby, any day now he can just show up, and we'll be good to go!"

Adam laughed as Piper dropped onto the desk chair and swiveled in a circle. "You can keep that baby in 'til mid-December, that way maybe you and Grayson can get married before the baby shows up."

"Yuck. I don't want to be pregnant another four weeks." Piper made a face. "I hate having to pee every five minutes, and I can't sleep. I know, I know, you don't sleep after you have a baby, either."

Adam had slept fine for the first two years after Piper was born, go figure.

Piper said, "Also, apparently the baby's going to be born with his clock backward so he wakes up around the time I want to go to bed, so from now on I've decided to stay up all night and sleep all day. I'll come to work at midnight and answer the phones then."

"Great idea." Adam snickered. "I sent you a few photos for

our social media, though, so if you could get those up now even though it's the unrealistic hour of eleven a.m., that would make your boss happy."

Piper logged in. "Would you mind if I don't marry Grayson as soon as he gets back?"

Adam stopped cold. "Why not?"

"Ella and I were talking. I'm not sure we should."

"Ella gave you cold feet?" Adam's brow furrowed. "Why would she say that?"

"Because Grayson and I didn't get to know each other long enough. We started dating, and then I got pregnant, and then he was out the door—and if we're going to be married forever, then putting it off six months doesn't matter much."

"Of course it matters! That baby needs a family." Adam came over to her desk. "Piper, honey, you've got to do what's best for the baby. He needs his father."

"Ella was saying, though, when you get married, you give your whole self to the other person, right?" Piper frowned. "She said I don't really know who I am right now, and when Grayson gets back, he won't really know who he is either because of everything he's been doing. And the baby of course doesn't know at all because he's just a baby."

Adam nodded. "Right. So you get married, and then when you're learning about the rest of you, whatever that means, you make the pieces fit together with each other so you work better together. You don't want to make this whole life for yourself and then start chopping pieces off of it to make someone else happy."

Frowning, Piper rubbed her belly. "That's what Mom always said. She didn't want to lose herself just because of some guy."

"Some guy" being Adam. Nice.

Adam folded his arms. "Your mother spent forty years wandering around trying to find herself, and I'm still not aware she's found it."

Piper's mouth trembled. "That's not fair."

"I don't think *yourself* is something you find. I've never pulled old boxes out of an attic and found someone's real self. But I have found a lot of garbage people crammed into their lives that they never needed in the first place." Adam glared at her. "Get married to Grayson, and then you two can grow up together."

Piper shook her head. "I don't know anymore. You say one thing and Mom says something else and Ella says something more, and—"

"Ella's not your mother." Adam glowered. "She's your midwife. You hired her. You can fire her."

Piper winked. "You could marry her, and then she'd be my mother."

"You don't need a mother. You've got one." Piper flinched, and Adam turned aside. "Ella wouldn't even be your stepmother because you're a grown adult. You can discount her advice except for how to give birth to your baby. Other than that, it's meddling."

"Dad!"

He walked out of the office, saying, "Marry Grayson, and tell her to quit interfering."

Among the furniture, Adam wrestled his thoughts into submission. Ella couldn't have said that. Piper was fully Kandace's daughter, and heaven knew Kandace always heard exactly what she wanted to hear.

Also, Ed always laughed that right before his own kids were born, his wife went nuts. Ed called it "nesting," and Adam would be lying if he said it wasn't good for business, too. The Junk Crew had oftentimes gotten an urgent call demanding they come shift a load of stuff out of a house, only to be met at the door by a hugely pregnant woman in tears because she needed to get the home cleared out before the baby arrived.

With it being the last few weeks now, he should expect Piper to get emotional about everything, including Grayson. More emotional, that was. Piper had never been number one in her class for self-restraint. If Ella didn't expect Piper to be having mood swings now, that didn't say much about her skill as a midwife.

The anger kept eating at him. After tagging several pieces for transport to the family shelter donation site, Adam pulled out his phone. "Piper says you told her not to get married."

Fifteen minutes later, probably between patients, Ella replied, "I didn't tell her not to get married. I told her not to rush if she wasn't sure."

Adam's eyes flared. "Why'd you tell her that?"

"Because for marriage, she should be sure."

"For having a baby, you should be sure," he texted. "That horse left the barn."

Ella replied, "This is true."

She was still replying though, so he waited on that. "It would get worse if she gets entangled in a bad marriage."

Adam started typing a reply, then deleted it. Because what would Ella know about bad marriages? She grew up in a family of professionals, married a guy who never worked with his hands a day in his life, and nowadays she got to live with his perfect ghost every day. Ella had no idea what it was like to live with instability.

Piper's baby needed a home. Adam's grandbaby needed two parents, and that baby needed to know when he woke up in the morning who'd be in the house and whether he'd go to sleep that night in the same bed.

Ella texted, "I don't know anything about Grayson, so I certainly wouldn't tell her not to marry him."

Maybe Grayson wasn't up to code. "Oh, the slats need to be an inch and a half apart, and a spouse needs to earn five grand a year more, plus his hair is too short." Adam should just keep an eye out for a new man whenever he did a haul. "Hey, are you getting rid of this perfectly good single mid-twenties guy? Mind if I repurpose him?"

Adam replied, "Well, that's what she heard."

Ella said, "Thanks for letting me know. I'll talk to her later and make sure she understands I'm not saying anything bad about

Grayson."

Ella was talking now like a midwife, not like his girlfriend, not like someone who cared about Piper's future. Adam shoved the phone in his pocket and went back to work.

Except then it buzzed again, so he checked it. Ella had texted, "Dinner tonight? I'll cook."

He replied, "Working late. I'm dropping off furniture at the family shelter."

It happened to be true, but he'd have said that anyway because right now he was too steamed to talk to Ella. Best give himself a day or two so he'd simmer down.

She texted, "Sorry, I forgot about that. I'll be free on Saturday. It looks like it's going to snow on Sunday."

"Sure." Maybe if he brought Ella back home for dinner, he could have the conversation again in front of Piper, and they could convince Piper to do the right thing.

Or, maybe he'd convince Ella to butt out of a situation she didn't belong in, because breaking up a marriage? That wasn't being "with woman." That was "instead of woman," and that wasn't right.

Chapter Fifteen

Ella exited her office at six o'clock. Adam was delivering that load of furniture, so the night was hers.

Lori was holding an animated conversation in the waiting room, and she waved Ella over. "You need to meet Tracy! She's one of our clients."

"Former client," the woman said with a laugh. "As I think I'm making perfectly clear."

"You're playing with fire." Lori raised her eyebrows. "Getting rid of the baby furniture is the most potent fertility drug known to humankind."

Ella shook Tracy's hand. She had a three-year-old on her hips and two older children playing with a plastic farm set in the corner. Tracy said, "I came by to drop off all the baby furniture in case you have any clients who can't afford what they need. It's all sturdy stuff. A changing table, a rocking chair, a dresser, a crib —the whole works."

Ella perked up. "I have a client whose crib isn't safe. She hasn't replaced it yet, and she's due any day now."

Lori nodded. "Perfect! We won't even bother bringing it in."

Five minutes later, the crib setup lay in the back of the Subaru station wagon. "She's going to love this." Ella was bouncing on her toes. "Thank you so much!"

How exciting! It was already full dark, but she wasn't hungry, so she might as well bring Piper the crib even though Adam wouldn't be there. Then Ella could take the chance to straighten things out about Grayson.

How could Piper have had that whole conversation and concluded that Ella didn't want her to get married? Misunderstandings happened, but Ella thought she'd been clear about "wait a bit" and not "dump the guy." There was no need to make Piper choose between getting married in four weeks versus never at all. If Piper was having those kind of second thoughts, she'd never indicated it. Best to suss that out now. Unnamed fears could impede delivery. Unvoiced anxiety could stall it out.

Ella's plan for tonight had been simple: go home, cook dinner, read, go to bed. She was on call, but her midwife instincts were telling her no one would need her. Therefore, she'd spend a half hour with Piper making sure they understood each other.

Adam was such a sweetheart, donating things that were good enough to sell. The shelter would tell him whenever a family was ready to move out, and he'd show up to their new apartment with a truck full of "good-enough-but-unwanteds." A sofa, some beds, a couple dressers, a bookshelf—and just like that, a building could become a home.

Are people like that, too?, Ella wondered as she slowed her car to bump her way over the railroad tracks. Maybe sometimes you felt "good enough but unwanted," until the moment you found the place you were wanted—and with that, you became a family and a home?

Ella had never been unwanted. Despite how half of Connecticut was glad to slam the door at her back, her family and friends had always wanted her. But too many times she'd counseled children at school who felt unwanted. Some of her clients felt unwanted. Her goal always was to make them feel not only wanted but welcomed. When their babies were born, she wanted those babies to enter into a world where they were welcomed with joy.

Piper met Ella on the porch, and Ella showed her the crib in the back of the car. "Perfect slats," Ella announced, and Piper squealed because the wood tone even matched the dresser. They hauled the pieces upstairs, then with help from all three dogs and one of the cats, they disassembled the old crib and reassembled the new one. The old crib just slid together with slots and grommets, but the new one had bolts and hex nuts. Piper was an ace with the tools.

"This is awesome!" Piper said, looking at the finished product. Then, "Oh, and this—less awesome." A blue blanket that did, indeed, proclaim, "Maverick."

The strain in Piper's eyes broke Ella's heart. "I'm sorry, honey. She doesn't get it."

"She does get it." Piper tossed the blanket back onto the rocking chair. "She picked a name, and I'm supposed to use it. Or else."

Ella said, "Okay, speaking of 'or else,' talk to me. Your father told me you don't want to marry Grayson?"

Piper turned to her. "What? I didn't say that. I said I was thinking about whether Grayson and I need to grow up a bit before we'll make a good family."

Adam had been clear over text, but it made Ella feel better to think the communication gap was between Adam and Piper, not between Piper and herself. "Your baby deserves a family, and I just want you to make sure your family has a firm foundation."

"Yeah, what you said makes sense. Dad wants me to marry Grayson like the minute he steps off the plane, but you're right it's a lot of changes all at once." She winked. "Let Grayson chase me for a bit, since he'll want a lot of snuggle time with his cute baby."

Ella laughed. "Now you're thinking!"

They replaced the mattress in the crib, re-did the sheets and the quilt (but not the Maverick blanket), and then carried the old crib parts back downstairs.

Piper said, "I'll stack these in the garage until I can drive them out to the dump. If it's not safe enough for my baby, then nobody's baby should be using it, right?" She turned to Ella. "Stick around for dinner! It's just American chop suey, but still."

"I don't want to bother you. Your dad deserves to decompress when he gets home."

Piper said, "Yeah, but you have to eat, and so does he!"

Ella pulled on her jacket. "I'll see your dad in a couple of days."

Piper blurted out, "Can you show me how a ring sling works? My mom sent me one with the blanket, and I can't figure it out."

The day had already been long, but the desperation in Piper's eyes drew Ella up short.

The sling was a simple model, a woven cotton rectangle with stitching strong enough to hold a suspension bridge and a pair of brass rings that clanked when they moved. Ella fed the sling tail through the rings, then set it crosswise on her body with the rings by her shoulder. "This is a nice one. I prefer these over the slings with the padded rails because you can't cinch them all the way."

Piper said, "Won't the baby fall out?"

"The rails aren't what keeps the baby in. Here." Ella set the sling on Piper, and then they got TJ, the world's most staid cat, and plunked him into the sling. Ella showed Piper how to tighten the rings, and now TJ was tucked up in the sling, looking confused but secure.

"See, you can move him up here," and she slid the contraption around so the cat had his head by Piper's shoulder. "You can slide him down, and you can see how if you have the baby this way, you could nurse in the sling in perfect privacy." She spread out the sling tail and covered the entire front of Piper's body. "If someone wants to touch your baby, you can drive them away." Ella flicked the sling tail like a whisk broom, and Piper laughed.

"Later on, you'll be able to swing the baby around to your back too."

"This is really cool! Thank you!" Piper handed Ella her phone. "Take a picture of me in it so I can show my mom."

As Ella photographed Piper and the sling-cat, the door opened behind her, and Adam came in. "Surprise." He sounded exhausted. "Well, I'm surprised. I thought I was seeing you tomorrow."

"She's showing me how to use a sling," Piper said, opening her hands to show off the put-upon cat. "And she brought me a new crib, too, so we got that set up."

Stopping dead in the entryway, Adam's eyes narrowed. "Are you kidding me?"

Ella said, "Someone donated it, and you hadn't found Piper a new one yet."

He stepped toward her. "You've been on my back about that crib since the day you walked in here. It's not good enough for you. Nothing is good enough for you."

Piper said, "Dad! That's not what she's saying!"

Adam said to Ella, "Then what are you saying? You replaced it because it was one hundred percent great? No—you hounded me about getting rid of something that's perfectly fine, and was perfectly fine for other people's kids, and when I didn't do it to your standards, you just went ahead and replaced it anyhow."

Breathless, Ella shook her head.

Adam said, "I get it, I'm not a doctor with a PhD, but I know how to assemble furniture. You don't have to go through life upgrading the first minute something better comes along."

Ella raised her hands. "It's not about upgrading. I'm going by the current guidelines."

Adam said, "You said your job isn't to force Piper to comply with the state. If you really think that baby's in jeopardy because the crib is twenty years old, you need to call child protective services and get the baby taken away from us as unfit parents."

Ella's eyes burned. "It's not about being unfit."

"It has everything to do with you standing in judgment over us and saying it's not good enough when you know full well it is. Piper was happy with that crib until you made her unhappy, just like she was happy with Grayson until you made her unhappy."

Piper wrung her hands. "I'm sorry! Dad, calm down. I didn't mean it. I'll put the other crib back up there."

Ella backed away. "I'll leave. I didn't think it was a big deal."

Adam said, "My family isn't a big deal to you. You want everything just so and think our family isn't right—and we're never a big deal. Not to you."

Biting her lip, Ella struggled not to lose composure.

Adam gestured to the door. "You were leaving?"

Piper said, "I don't want her to go! She's been helping me!"

"Helping? She's telling you not to get married. She wants your baby tossed back and forth like a football, nothing ever good enough. The crib's not good enough, and the car seat isn't good enough, and Grayson isn't good enough." He pivoted back toward Ella. "How long until Piper isn't good enough either? But what if in actuality we're all exactly good enough—and it's only the judge who isn't good enough?"

Ella went to the door, head ringing and eyes blurry. A cold rain lay slick on the driveway, and she sat with the windshield wipers going for half a minute before she dared put the car in gear. She didn't want to drive in this state, but she also didn't want to sit in Adam's driveway crying.

Chapter Sixteen

In the morning, Piper dragged around with red eyes and shoulders hunched.

No matter how often Adam said it wasn't her fault, Piper wore a hangdog expression over breakfast, didn't want to talk while she rode with him to work, and kept trying to anticipate everything he needed once they got to the warehouse.

It only made him angrier at Ella. Piper was taking all this blame on herself when the real problem was Ella messing with things she had no right meddling with. Like Piper getting married to Grayson. Like furniture. Ella needed to do her medical stuff and keep quiet about the rest of it. A doctor wouldn't go inspect the house. A doctor would say, "You got a crib? Good."

Piper had wanted to play matchmaker, and now she was blaming herself for that, too, because if she hadn't gotten Adam and Ella together, they couldn't have broken up.

This morning's schedule had Adam and two guys in one of the larger trucks out at the storage units on 1A. Right before he got in the truck, Piper came to him with his thermos. "Here." She sounded subdued. "I thought you'd like to bring some coffee."

Adam took it. "Honey, quit beating yourself up over everything. It's not your fault."

She shrugged, and obviously she didn't believe him. "I just thought you'd like coffee."

Piper looked like she needed coffee. He had no idea if she'd she'd been awake all night texting Grayson. Or for that matter, texting Ella.

Out at the storage units, the manager gave Adam the keys to the three abandoned units. "Anything you find is yours. Unless you find a bin full of diamonds. That's mine." The guy laughed. "Just kidding. I already checked them all."

Storage unit clean-outs were easy money in the bank. Most of the time was just like this, where management had already gone in and cleared out everything that might be worth anything, so Adam treated it all as garbage. He'd bill by the load, and no one needed to waste even a second wondering if something could be salvaged.

Sometimes people paid Adam to load their storage cubes for them, and he was waiting for the day he got paid to trash out that same storage cube. No one valued their stuff. Why keep something when they could grab something new? But then they couldn't exactly get rid of the old thing, either. Security, at the expense of storage space.

Adam unlocked the first unit, muttering, "People should just get rid of what they don't need instead of saving it ten years."

Behind him, one of his crew snickered. "Yeah, but I like having a job."

They backed up the truck to the unit and chucked in everything. Boxes of mildewed clothes, blankets, a dresser with half the drawers busted, generic paintings that had rotted out: it felt good to toss them all into the truck. Focused on the work, Adam let it go through him: the hefting, the hauling, the heaving. With no decisions to make, he closed off his brain.

Piper was so upset.

Piper didn't want to change to a different practice, so Adam was just going to have to hope it wasn't Ella on call when Piper's time came.

Well, they could work together for a few hours, at least. Ella would pass judgment on them and all their things, that his boiling water wasn't boiling enough for code, but the birth was Ella's show. Raising that baby was Piper's show. Raising Piper was his.

One storage unit down, two to go.

One of the guys said, "I hope the other two units aren't crammed as full as this one. We might need two trips."

"We'll get it in one." Amazing what you could stuff into a fifteen-foot hauler. Amazing how much parenting you could force into random weekends here and there.

The second unit wasn't as bad as the first. Everything was in boxes, so it went fast. Management had slit open a couple at the front, but they hadn't ransacked them looking for valuables. All three men had their jackets off but their work gloves on. They could see their breath, but they were all working hot.

Third unit, completely full of black trash bags. Adam started tossing them out to his guys, and after four bags, exclaimed, "Are you kidding?"

Buried in the detritus was a snowmobile.

"Dibs," said one of the guys.

"I don't think so." Adam sighed. "Okay, we figure that one out later. The rest of it, into the truck."

They loaded the snowmobile onto the back of Adam's pickup truck, and Adam handled the tiedowns. Having a load like that shift in traffic was a bad idea—it had to weigh over four hundred pounds.

As Adam attached the ratchet straps in the rear of the snowmobile, he thought about how exact he was being with this load. How this was his job, and he knew what he was doing.

If he saw Ella transporting something large like this without tying it down, he'd say something. Of course he would. "That's dangerous." He wouldn't let her onto the highway with the back end of the snowmobile hanging over the edge and no tiedown bar in the front of the bed to secure it in place. He'd jump in to stop her if she tried to attach the straps to plastic instead of to steel.

So her with the crib, maybe that was the same way? Maybe she saw a crib and thought, "That baby could get its head trapped," the same way he saw a snowmobile and thought, "That load could shift once it's up to speed."

That still didn't give her the right to tell Piper not to get married.

Or maybe it did. Maybe she looked at Piper and thought, "That marriage could shift if it's not tied down properly. That baby could get its heart trapped between two parents who can't work together."

Adam slapped the snowmobile. That thing wasn't going anywhere.

Ella hadn't texted since yesterday. He hadn't expected her to. She'd survived the death of a marriage, so she had all the skills in place to survive the death of a six-week dating relationship. Her fridge probably had cheese older than that. She survived an entire town hating her, so Adam's anger wouldn't even register. Once Piper delivered, Ella would drop the cast-offs of whatever he and she had together, and she'd move on. Adam could once again stand in the junk, looking at the unwanted remains that got left behind.

Every time Kandace had rejected him, it had been for no reason. She'd found excuses not to stick around, not to accept his help, not to work with him to parent Piper. Nothing he did was good enough because she'd never wanted it to be good enough. How could it have been? Kandace wanted something or someone else to make her happy. A boyfriend? A baby? A new lover? A new state? A new job? But time after time after time, she was never happy, and she'd ask for more. She'd say it was his fault she was never happy. She'd always raise the bar, raise the stakes, raise the expectations.

Then Ella walked in and said, "That crib isn't up to code," and bam, it was Kandace all over again. Nothing's ever good enough, and Ella would just go ahead and take care of it herself because Adam wasn't fit to raise a baby. That was how Adam was hearing it, but what was she actually saying? What if she was actually saying, "That crib isn't up to code"?

What if she wasn't saying, "Piper, you should jerk around Grayson just like your mom jerked around your father"? Maybe she was actually saying, "Marriage is a big deal, and you're practically a kid."

She'd told Piper that if Piper didn't know herself real well yet, then how could Piper give all of herself to someone else? The obvious next question was how Adam could give all of himself to someone else if part of him had never slipped out of the choke-chain Kandace had set around his neck. He thought he was fighting with Ella, but really he was fighting with Kandace —or the part of him that believed everything Kandace ever said about him.

He walked to his guys standing at the cab of the hauler. "You can haul everything over to the dump."

One of the guys flexed his shoulders. "That snowmobile's a beauty. I'm thinking some people throw away good stuff, and they never even know it."

That hit close to home. Adam walked back into the storage unit to make sure everything was bare inside those metal walls. He said to himself, "And I'm thinking, for someone who hates junk, I sure carry a lot of baggage."

He hung the lock back on the door.

Chapter Seventeen

The text conversation with Piper went this way:

I'm so sorry that happened! I had no idea Dad would go off like that.

It's okay. It's fine, and if you want to switch the cribs, I'll take back the new one.

No, it's not fine, and I'm so sorry. I don't know what to do.

Don't be sorry, and I want you not to stress. The baby needs his mom calm and happy.

I blew everything up between you two and that's horrible and I'm so sorry.

Over and over, it was just Ella telling Piper to breathe, to relax, to get some sleep, to disengage. No, it wasn't her fault. The important issues were Piper and her baby, and now was the time for calm.

Slipping into her professional groove helped. It also helped when Ella got a midnight call with a client uncertain if she was in early labor. "It wouldn't surprise me," Ella said. "It's nearly the new moon, plus there's a storm heading in. But it doesn't sound like your contractions are productive right now, so rest for an hour, get some fluids, and call me back." An hour later, the woman called back: the painless contractions had stopped, and she was going to bed.

The next day, it helped when Ella worked through a full schedule in the office. Piper had gone radio silent. Adam hadn't texted, nor had she expected him to. What would she say that she hadn't already? Her job was protecting babies and mothers. Piper's life was rough enough without the nightmare of finding her baby trapped in the crib bars.

After surviving the loss of Brett, Ella could survive losing Adam. She just needed to come up with a schedule and a checklist of things to do—and her profession provided all that.

Ella moved through her day, keeping her appointments on time, getting her numbers in order and making sure she ticked through all the boxes. Her late-night caller came in for a visit, but after they talked fifteen minutes, Ella decided nothing was happening on the labor front. "I can check dilation if you want," she offered, but the mom didn't want it, so off she went. It was just as well. Ella counted it a victory every time a client delivered without having any internal exams after the first visit.

Ella worked through lunch, only drinking coffee between clients. She wasn't hungry.

Adam's accusations weren't fair. Calling it "meddling" when she was doing the job Piper had brought her onboard to do— that wasn't fair. Piper needed her. Piper had switched to a brand-new practice in the third trimester because her previous obstetric practice had been demanding and unyielding. *Yes, she had to follow their schedule. No, she could not decline their procedures. Yes, she would be having her membranes stripped at 38 weeks. No, she could not refuse it. No, she could not refuse internal exams in the last month.* On and on and on.

Midwife meant "with woman," Ella kept saying, so she was going through the last weeks of the pregnancy with Piper. If Adam objected, then Adam was the one with the problem.

Brett would never have done this. Brett didn't interfere with Ella doing her job. Everyone knew they were married, of course, and sometimes parents with children in both schools would complain to him about her. "Can't you stop her from calling me at work to take my kid home just because he's vomiting?" Brett would reply, "I am not in charge of doing my wife's job. You'll have to speak to her about it."

Meanwhile, Brett would laugh with her about the kids' antics, like the students who used those portable hand-warmers on their foreheads. "Wow, despite a fever of 118, I think you can make it through the rest of the day." At the same time, when she'd encountered a serious case of neglect, he'd let her handle it even though several parents complained that she was being unfair—as though she had anything at all to do with what child protective services decided.

Brett respected her work. He didn't say, "Well, you're only a nurse, so quit interfering in families' lives by chasing down the medical records required by the state."

Five years ago, she'd accepted that she'd never find another Brett, but did it really have to be so different?

Piper didn't text again in the afternoon. Ella went home and forced herself to eat a sandwich for dinner. Eventually she picked a movie she'd watched ten times already and sat in front of the TV with *The Eternal Sunshine of the Spotless Mind* on the screen and half a knitted dishcloth in her lap.

Dishcloths were good. If you followed the directions for the stitches, you ended up with something that made dishes clean.

Ella hadn't been knitting long. One of her husband's nurses had taught her, as a way of keeping her hands busy at the bedside. Ella could count stitch by stitch and do anything rectangular, but she had to focus, and focus was what she needed. The nurse who'd taught her had been one of those people who'd pick up a pair of sticks and a skein of anything and just whip a mitten pattern out of her head. You'd be talking to her about schedules, and she'd be making a thumb.

"Aren't you worried about making mistakes?" Ella had asked.

The nurse just laughed. "Mistakes become design elements, and they make the piece truly yours. In fact, most of the things you do to make lace are fancy planned mistakes."

Ella had laughed and stuck to dishcloths. Tonight, she didn't laugh.

It wasn't fair. She'd been getting close to Adam. He'd been making her smile, and he'd been doing such nice things for her. No, of course he wasn't Brett. He didn't have to be Brett though. If the competition were to see who got to be the best Brett, Brett would always win. Adam had to be Adam.

Adam had to let Ella be Ella. Part of Ella was Ella's job, and Ella's job was looking out for Piper. Once she realized Piper's crib wasn't safe, Ella needed to get her to replace it. If Piper's relationship wasn't safe, Ella needed to warn her. All of that made sense. Midwife. "With woman." Piper wanted Ella with her. How much simpler did it get?

Ella got to the end of the row, and she didn't turn. She closed her eyes, and she stopped.

Piper needed Ella "with her" to assist her in the things she decided to do. Ella's job wasn't to make the decisions. It was to guide, warn, assess—and ultimately, be *with*. But not to drive the decisions. Not to insist. Not to direct.

Warning her about the crib? That was fine. Not allowing that particular crib into the midwifery center nursery would have been fine, but Ella had no jurisdiction over Piper's home. Asking if Piper had concerns about her relationship? Very much encouraged. Telling her to marry or not marry? That was a massive overstep.

Not that she'd told her not to marry Grayson. She'd just given Piper questions to think about, and Piper may have used that as an excuse she needed.

Except… It was more, wasn't it? Piper wanted Ella together with her father. To some extent, that meant she'd framed Ella as a mother, and what did Piper do? Piper listened to her mother.

Ella muted the TV but left it playing. Okay. Think. Think hard. What had she said and done? Because if she was truly stepping into the role of surrogate mother—*stepping in* as mother to someone who didn't need a stepmother—then Adam was right.

Piper didn't want that new crib. She'd been excited to get it, but if Ella had driven across the railroad tracks to bring Piper a handknit dishcloth, Piper would have responded exactly same way. Piper's mother had given love so inconsistently that anything was a gift. Listening was love. Attention was devotion. Suggestions were directives.

Adam was right.

If Ella had truly been "with Piper," then she would have known how Piper was hearing her. All along, Ella had said Piper was a young mother who was driving the decisions about how to best parent her baby, while at the same time ignoring that Piper was a young woman who still needed her mother. If nothing else, Ella should have realized it when Piper was so upset about not being able to use the ring sling just because her mother expected her to use it. Or the hassle about the baby's name. Piper's mother hadn't given her the really important things throughout the pregnancy—advice, encouragement, experiences—and now she'd sent her a $35 piece of cloth and brass, so Piper would seize on that as love.

"With Piper" would mean walking the road at Piper's side and letting her choose the path. It didn't mean walking ahead and yanking her by the hand or walking behind and steering her shoulders.

All those guidelines and rules, those were meant to protect Ella as a practitioner. She had to make the statement about the crib. Once. She had to ask if the relationship was safe. She had to hand Piper the pamphlet about car seats and make sure she had one properly installed. Then Ella had to step back.

The rules had kept Ella safe until now. Rules about who orders first, when to change careers after a death, how to file a lawsuit, how to start a new life in another state. But as that knitting nurse had said, deviating from the rules made your project your own. Not only that, but strategically stacking the planned deviations ended up creating beauty.

Ella turned the dishcloth and kept knitting. She left the TV muted, but the pictures flickered in the corner of her eye. She'd have to see Adam again when Piper delivered.

Were there rules about how to apologize? Because she had to apologize first to Piper, and then to him.

Chapter Eighteen

With six inches of snow on the ground Saturday night, Ella got the text she expected. "I think I'm in labor."

Lori was with another laboring mom because storms always brought babies. Ella couldn't have handed this off if she wanted to, but she didn't want to. Instead Ella paced to her window and hit the button to call Piper back.

"Hey." Piper sounded uneasy. "I know it's early, but I'm worried."

"That's fine. I don't want you to be worried." How much of this was worry, and how much of this was Piper trying to force Ella and Adam back together? "Tell me what you're feeling."

"Remember you said about the contractions wrapping around to the back of me? And also, they're lower." Piper gave Ella a list of symptoms that might have come from the "Am I in Labor?" handout at the 32-week visit. How often were they coming? About every five minutes. Ella checked the time. She'd keep Piper on the phone long enough that Piper had to talk through one of them.

"What have you been eating today?" Ella said, and in the middle of listing off everything since breakfast, Piper hesitated.

"Oh, that was another one," and the note in her voice told Ella this was the real thing.

"How long has this been going on?" Half an hour.

Ella again looked out the window at the snow. The weather wasn't kidding around. The overnight totals were predicted up to eighteen inches.

First labors, though—they could last twenty-four hours or even longer.

Timing your arrival as a midwife was a balance. Having a midwife camped out in the living room would make a laboring mom feel as though she were on the clock. By the same token, a new mom laboring without her midwife might angst about what would happen if the midwife didn't make it in time.

All that was beside the question of how Adam would deal with having Ella in his living room for an excessive number of hours. She'd known they would have to talk at some point, but that didn't mean they had to camp in the same room for twenty-four hours.

Ella said, "Here's what I'm thinking, and I want your opinion. I can come right now if you want me there to assess you and the baby and make sure everything is okay." Piper had already said the baby was moving well, so if she chose this option, it would be just because Piper needed reassurance. "If the action is still early for you, I could come home and then return when you're closer to time."

Piper said, "You normally want to get here when I'm in active labor, right? And this sounds like early labor?"

"You've never been in labor before, so if you want me to check you, I will check you." Ella worked to keep her voice neutral. "I will come the instant you say the word. If you don't want me to come, then what I'll have you do is time your contractions for the next hour and then call me back. Either way, I'd want you to lie down in bed."

Piper said, "What if I fall asleep?"

Ella chuckled. "That would be perfect because it would mean

more rest before the really hard part of the delivery."

"Oh." Piper perked up. "I was more afraid like I'd wake up with contractions every sixty seconds and you couldn't get here in time."

Glancing out the window, Ella shivered. It would be at least a half hour's drive to their house, only getting longer as the roads got worse. The plow crews were already sanding and salting, growling their way down the streets as they pushed the snow to the side. "I doubt you'd doze through active labor, although there are tall tales about moms who delivered healthy babies in their sleep."

Piper exclaimed, "That can happen?"

"Only if you're supremely lucky."

This time Piper's laugh did sound relaxed. "Let's try that, then. I'll hang out in the hot tub and watch the clock."

An hour later, Piper was back on the phone. "They're still four minutes apart, and I am not getting out of this tub for a million dollars," and she talked through a contraction just fine. Ella set an alarm for another hour and dozed off fully clothed with her bag packed and her phone in her hand.

Fifty minutes after that, Piper called, sounding wobbly. "Can you come now?" and Ella went out the door.

The snow was intense. With the Subaru in four-wheel drive and defroster blowing at full bore, Ella crawled along the barely-plowed side streets until she reached the main road, but at least there the plows had managed to keep up. Her wipers swiped as fast as they could, the snow luminescent in her headlights as she crept forward through town.

Halfway through Hartwell, the streetlights blinked out. The houses at the side of the road were dark. All dark. Everything, out.

Two minutes later, as Ella got out of town, a text came from Adam. "Power's out."

With both hands on the wheel, Ella couldn't answer. What would she even have said? *Tell Piper to reschedule her delivery for sometime more convenient for the power company."* Piper had wanted to birth in the hot tub, though, and Ella had been gearing up for exactly that kind of birth. On the other hand, although Piper would lose the jets, the water in the tub would stay warm for hours. The power crews worked pretty fast. Knowing this storm would be a big one, they were probably already at work.

Ella rounded the curve to the railroad tracks and found the road blocked by a train. She waited, but the train didn't move.

It was possible to get past the train if she went the long way around the horseshoe. She texted Adam, "A train's stopped on the tracks. I'm coming via Northwoods Road."

At the crossing on Northwoods Road, Ella found the road blocked by the same train, still stopped. Not only stopped, but with snowcaps on every available surface, and all over the tracks.

Enough of texting. She called. Adam answered.

"We have a problem. It looks like the freight train is wrapped entirely around the horseshoe, and it hasn't moved in ten minutes."

Her wipers swished in a rapid rhythm. The snow was only coming down faster, and the hood of her car was already covered.

Adam said, "Piper's holding up good so far, but I'm going to bring her into the house because we can't keep the tub warm."

"Early labor can go a long time," Ella said. "How long does it normally take to get a train out of here?"

"Trains don't usually get stuck there. I can keep checking it and call you if it moves."

In the background she heard. "Is that Ella?"

Piper sounded scared. Piper wanted her.

Talking away from the phone, Adam sounded muffled. "The train's blocking the road at both ends. She can't get past."

Softer conversation, and then Adam was talking to Ella again. "She'll be all right. You go home, and I'll call when it's clear."

Ella put her car back in gear and crawled back toward

Hartwell. Out this far, plows were scarcer. If she went into a ditch, the car was staying for an hour.

A text popped up from Adam. "I loaded a scanner app to catch the railroad chatter. The train's stuck. Go home."

Ella returned to the first railroad crossing where the train remained exactly where it had been. Well, now her car could join it. With the flexible flashlight wrapped around her neck and her bag strapped around her body, she unplugged her phone to text Adam. "I'm walking in."

The phone rang in her hand. She answered with, "I can get between the cars and then follow the road."

"Are you out of your mind?"

"You said that train isn't moving. If there were a danger that the train would move, I'd wait in my car, but since you're saying it's stuck, I can climb through, and then I'll follow the road. I know where you live."

"You're going to wander into the woods and die," Adam said. "Get back in your car. I'll call an ambulance and bring her to the hospital if I have to."

"An ambulance can't get through any better than I can. You'll need a helicopter." She got out of the car. "The snow isn't that bad. I have a flashlight, and if I bump into a tree, I'll get back to the cleared areas."

He said, "There aren't even street lights!"

She hung up on him.

It wasn't difficult to climb between the train cars, and then Ella started hiking. The wind swirled snow into her face and stung her cheeks, but she'd bundled up well, her scarf over her cheeks, her hat down low, her gloved hands in her pockets. With no plows getting past the train, five inches of snow had accumulated. She was pushing through it with every step, but thanks to her flashlight around her neck, it wasn't hard to follow the road.

Well, until the moment it was hard to follow. Either it curved, and a driveway went straight off it, or else it went straight, and the curve was a driveway.

Blast. She fumbled her phone out of her pocket, hoping the GPS would at least identify where the road went. Except now the screen was wet with the snow, and her fingers were wet, and the touch screen wouldn't respond. She took five tries even to wake up the phone, and then she couldn't get the map app to respond.

A whine approached, like a motor. A very small motor, that was. The snow absorbed most of the sound, but then Ella saw light approaching on the curving road. A vehicle? If so, it was probably on the real road. Maybe she should wave down the driver? At the very least, the person needed to know a train was blocking the road.

It wasn't a pair of headlights, though. Or maybe two headlights very close together. That wasn't a motorcycle, was it?

As it grew louder, it resolved into a snowmobile. Ella hurried off the road.

The driver pulled up to her, though, and raised his goggles. Adam. "I said you'd wander off the road, and you were about to get lost. Get on."

"I didn't get off the road until I was trying to avoid the snowmobile." She couldn't figure out exactly how to mount the thing, so she just climbed up behind him. There wasn't much seat space. This couldn't possibly be safe—not with her not wearing a helmet—actually, neither was he—and no seat belt, no nothing. "You shouldn't have left Piper."

"Piper has the dogs and was ranting at me to go get you. You're just lucky I have one of these things."

Ella wrapped her arms around his waist. "If she's ranting, she's not close to delivering."

Adam started the snowmobile. "You have the weirdest outlook." As he began turning, he said, "Tuck your face behind my back. It's going to get windy."

She held tight to her equipment bag and closed her eyes for the ride.

It was loud. It was frigid. It was nice to have her arms around Adam, but at the same time it hurt because she'd treated him badly—and yet he'd still come out in the snow to find her.

Then the motor eased up, and they turned in to the long driveway in front of the bungalow. Shaking, Ella tried to figure out how to get down, but then Adam dismounted and helped her to her feet again on solid ground. "You okay?"

No, she wasn't okay. Her knees were trembling, and her face was numb. She clutched her bag all the tighter, avoiding his eyes. "I'd better be. I have a baby to deliver."

In the house, Ella found Piper leaning over the couch, one dog on either side. Moonie growled, but even though Piper looked teary-eyed, she steadied her. "Ella!" She started to get up, then flinched with her eyes closed.

"Oh, you're going good." Ella rushed for her, not even taking off her jacket before she had Piper in her arms and a contraction took her. "Honey, breathe deep and long. I've only been here for thirty seconds, and I can see you're doing great."

Piper whined at her, and Ricky leaned against them both. Ella counted off the seconds, and finally the contraction ended. She got Piper settled, then unzipped her jacket. Adam lifted it off her before she was even out of the sleeves, then took her hat and scarf which were already dripping. The house was warm. This must be the only room with heat, but boy was that woodstove taking care of business. Adam had set flashlights all around, plus candles on the mantle with a mirror behind them.

Ella started rubbing Piper's lower back. "Remember when I told you to be flexible about your birth plan?"

Piper wailed, "I didn't want to have to be this flexible!" and then she gasped.

Contractions were two minutes apart. Definitely active labor. Ella still needed to apologize to Adam, but right now, Piper needed Ella.

Chapter Nineteen

Adam had no idea what to do with himself, so he sat with Piper and held her hands while she endured the contractions. He kept telling her to hang in there, and he'd remind her to breathe the same way Ella was reminding her, but Piper was crying. Ella kept helping her find different positions to labor in. She was on her knees in front of the rocking chair right now, face down on her folded arms, and whenever the contractions came, she'd rock from her hips.

The power didn't come back. Sometimes, Adam fed the fire. Ricky and Moonie were with them, uneasy but tolerant of Ella's presence and Piper's distress. TJ the cat sat on the back of the pull-out couch, watching. Ella kept getting the baby's heartbeat, then making notes. "Everything's fine," she kept saying, but the longer the night went, the less positive she sounded.

Ella stroked Piper's hair. She rubbed her shoulders. Piper wanted physical contact—lots of it. She wanted her father's hugs, and she wanted Ella to massage her back, and then a contraction would come and she wanted it all to stop.

Adam couldn't even brew a pot of coffee.

At three o'clock, Ella went into the kitchen, and from the

doorway, she signaled to him. Piper had just finished a contraction, so they had two minutes. Adam went to her. "You want something?"

Ella pulled him into the kitchen. "Her labor is stalled, and I don't know why. When I got here, she was in active labor, and she should be in transition by now. She's not making progress."

Adam's brow furrowed. "Is that dangerous?"

"The baby is fine, but I don't want her to wear herself out. Something's stopping her, and I'm going to do everything I can, but—" Ella looked up at him. "You're right that I was meddling before."

Adam said, "No, I—"

"Quit it and listen to me before she needs us again. I was meddling, and I shouldn't have. I'm sorry. But what I'm about to do now is going to go so far beyond meddling that you won't even have the words for it."

Adam's eyes narrowed. "Don't you dare hurt her."

"If I hurt her, you do whatever you have to. Something's blocking her. I've been doing everything I can to rule out a physical issue, so I'm about to go deeper."

Piper called, and Ella ran to her. So tense he was shaking, Adam followed.

His daughter. His grandson. And this woman who had all the control and apparently no compunction about using it.

Ella put her arms around Piper in the twi-darkness of a room lit with candles and flashlights, and she soothed her through the contraction. Then, as the contraction eased off, Ella said, "Piper, sweetie, do you trust me?"

Adam's fists clenched. "Ella—"

"Piper," Ella breathed in her ear, "I need you to tell me. The thing you don't want to say out loud, I need you to tell it to me. Before the baby's born, you need to say it out loud."

Piper wrapped her arms around Ella and buried her face in Ella's shoulder. Ella soothed her, running a hand over her hair.

Adam moved nearer and laid a hand on his daughter. "Piper,

you don't have to say anything you don't want to."

Piper's voice broke in a sob. "I'm so sorry. I can't do this."

"Of course you can do this." Adam grabbed her hand where she was clutching Ella's shoulder. "You know you can do this."

"I'm so sorry."

She kept repeating how sorry she was, and Ella rocked her. The next contraction came, and Piper began bawling.

His daughter needed a hospital. She needed an epidural and eight hours of sleep. He should call and see if they could get an ambulance through somehow. At least get the ambulance to the other side the tracks and figure out how to get Piper past the train.

As the contraction ebbed, Ella said, "We're so proud of you."

Piper broke down. "No, you're not! I'm letting you down. I'm letting everybody down. It's all my fault, and I can't. I made Dad sad and I made you sad and I'm doing it all wrong—all of it, all of it."

Adam said, "Sweetheart! You didn't make me sad."

"I let you down! I didn't get married, and the crib, and the baby, and everything."

Ella had her eyes riveted to Adam. He didn't even need the prompting. "Piper, listen to me. I am so proud of you. You've done so much. You did everything. You're brave and smart and strong, and you're going to have this baby, and you're going to raise him, and as soon as you hold him, you're going to see how I feel. Your baby won't ever be able to do anything to make you stop loving him."

Piper choked, "Mom doesn't love me."

Adam grabbed her out of Ella's arms, and that was it. The dam went down, and Piper sobbed into his shoulder just like when she was a little girl—only these were the words she'd never said in all those years. *Mom doesn't love me.* The words kept tumbling out of her—how she'd lost her mother's love by growing up, and now she was going to lose her father too because she'd upset him, and she was upsetting Ella, and everything was a disaster. She was going to have the baby and lose everything. Everything.

Adam kept soothing her through the next contraction. When she settled again, he said, "Piper, I promise you. I promise you with everything I have, I love you, and I will always be here for you. You will always be my daughter. I will always be your father. I will never give up on you."

She whimpered, "Mom gave up on me."

He looked at Ella for any indicator what to say next, but Ella did nothing. She'd said the thing he needed to do during the birth was be Piper's father. She wasn't going to tell him how.

Piper breathed, "Mom gave birth alone. She said I didn't need help. I should just do it. Be strong enough by myself. She hated that I was going to a doctor. She hates that I'm weak. She hates Ella, too. I let her down. She gave up on me."

It had been a while between contractions. Catching Ella's gaze, Adam tightened his eyes, then glanced at his watch. She raised a hand and nodded. Okay, so she'd noticed. But what did that mean? The point was to un-stall labor, not stop it completely.

Adam said, "Honey, your mother has problems. I never understood her, but I won't give up. You do whatever you have to do. I'm going to be here."

Ella spoke for the first time in a while. "Your mom isn't you. Think about what you know. You're strong enough to ask for help when you need it. You're strong enough to listen to advice and figure out what works best. You're strong enough to believe in your father. You're strong enough to be your own person."

Piper reached for Ella's hand, and she just held it. Adam watched, wide eyed.

With woman. Ella had gotten past Piper's defenses, uncovered her fear, and shown her a way forward. Having her baby meant losing her mother, so Piper had been fighting herself. She'd struggled to get herself a new mother, and now she teetered on the brink of losing everyone. Her birth mother. The mother-figure she'd chosen. And, also, her father.

"I'm proud of you, too," Ella murmured, stroking Piper's hair. "You're not going to lose your dad because of any choices you make tonight. He's a good man. All you have to do is show up, and he's going to love you. You're not going to lose me, either. I'm here for you, no matter what. And you know what? You're going to be a great mom."

Piper lay slack in Adam's arms until the next contraction came, but she wasn't crying any longer. Even Adam could see she was working better with her own body, and her baby would come by dawn.

Chapter Twenty

Dawn began breaking, but the room was still dark. Piper had gone through transition with significantly less pain than her active labor. Ella had even gotten her to eat some soup, and then her contractions had stopped.

Wonderful. Dilation was complete, and Piper's body was resting while the baby kept descending. In a few minutes, the baby would get low enough to trigger her pushing reflex, but until then, Piper cold get a breather, have a sports drink, and ready herself for the third stage of labor.

Piper said, "Should I get out of my leggings now?"

Ella said, "You'd make your midwife very happy if you did," and Piper laughed. She was wearing a tremendous sleep shirt over her leggings, and she stayed in that while stripping from the waist down. Adam had no idea where to look, so Ella suggested, "Stay behind her, and look over her shoulder."

Uncomfortable, he said, "Yeah, that might be best."

Piper snickered. "I'm sure you changed my diapers. Oh!" Her eyes widened, and she pushed.

Ella went to work. She'd already spread a shower curtain on the carpet, and she yanked on a pair of nitrile gloves. "You've got this!" she shouted. "Good work!"

Piper pushed through the contraction, sweating, then collapsed back onto her father. She was pushing in a C position, rocked back on her tailbone with her legs propped before her, her back against her father's chest.

"Baby definitely moved down." Ella aimed her neck light for better visibility. "Push whenever you feel like it. When the urge stops, you stop. If you can get three pushes per contraction, that's great. If not, don't force it."

Adam rubbed Piper's shoulder. "Hon, when you're pushing, breathe to let out your air. Make noises. Sound like you're pushing a refrigerator across a carpet."

Ella laughed. Adam raised his eyebrows. "Hey, if I know anything, I know about lifting and pushing."

Piper laughed, too. Ella prompted, "Did it feel good to push?"

Piper exclaimed, "That felt mighty!" and Ella squeezed her hand.

Every time Piper pushed, she curved over herself, but she had her hands clenched in her father's. The baby kept descending, and Ella kept encouraging her. She checked through a contraction, and the baby's heartbeat was strong the whole time. Piper changed positions to push while kneeling, facing her father. Her water broke. She started complaining about that ring-of-fire burn, and Ella broke open the thermal packs to warm the baby blankets.

Ella exclaimed, "Look at that head of hair!" and Piper groaned as she pushed again. She flipped back into a C position, and Ella changed position to accommodate. "You've got this! He's nearly out!"

Piper pushed again, rocked back on her tailbone, and the baby's head emerged. "Awesome work!" Except then the contraction quit.

Ella's intuition screamed at her, and she aimed her flashlight at the baby. His skin was dusky, not pink, and she checked his heartbeat. It was in the nineties. Too slow.

"Piper!" Her voice was low. "Push. Now."

"I don't have—."

"Push!"

Piper did push, but nothing happened.

Ella grabbed Piper's ankles and shoved her knees back to her ears. "Again! We need him out of there."

Piper tried, but the contraction was done, and she couldn't make any progress.

Ella stuck her finger in alongside the baby's neck. She couldn't feel the shoulder, but she could feel the cord. Pinched.

The baby wasn't getting oxygen through the cord, and his shoulder was stuck behind the pelvic bones.

Ella said, "When you get that next contraction, you're going to have to push harder than you've ever done."

Piper exclaimed, "What's wrong?"

"Get up on hands and knees. We need him out of there."

Piper moved faster than anyone would think possible with a head between her legs, Ella reversing the whole layout in her head as Piper moved. Piper groaned again as she pushed, vocalizing as loud as possible while Ella tried to get a grip on the baby. The baby budged, and she finally felt that shoulder. She hooked a finger under it, trying to rotate him. "Piper, again!"

She let out a shout like a black belt. Adam was holding her shoulders, but he was watching Ella.

"Piper, get on your side." Ella flipped Piper sideways and pushed her upper leg straight into the air. Flagpole position. "Shoulder dystocia. Next contraction, we're getting him out." The baby's head was out, but he wasn't breathing. The little hairs under his nose weren't moving. He was just getting grayer.

Ella pulled out her ambubag. She set the mask over the baby's nose and mouth and gave him a couple of quick pumps. His heart rate was still falling.

New contraction. Piper pushed with her leg straight in the air, and Adam helped hold it up. Ella got the baby rotated a bit more, but then Piper flipped back onto her hands and knees and leaned way forward as she pushed again—and out slid the baby.

Ella laid the baby flat on the warmed towels, right alongside his mother.

Emergency. Triage.

First, take five seconds to assess.

Heartbeat, sixty. Breaths per minute, none. Skin tone, dark blue. Muscle tone, floppy.

Severe asphyxia.

She unwound the cord from around the baby's neck and armpit. Next, she grabbed the nearest warm blanket and wrapped him up. That done, she used the suction bulb to clear his mouth and nose.

He didn't choke or gag. He lay limp, unbreathing.

Piper struggled to prop herself up. "What's going on? What's happening?"

"He's not breathing," Ella said. "Adam, check the time."

With the baby's head at her knees, Ella replaced the ambubag mask over his face and gave another three puffs. She set that aside and opened the blanket. Tactile stimulation first, running her hands down his chest to stimulate that first breath. Then a quick rub of the feet. It had been at least a minute by now.

Strip the cord. Ella grasped the umbilical cord and ran her fingers along its length toward the baby. That was his blood. It had his oxygen. Get as much oxygenated blood into his body as possible, and it would give him that much more time before he needed to breathe.

Tears streamed down Piper's face as she lay on her side facing her son. Ella said, "Adam, time?"

He said, "Two minutes, ten seconds."

Come on, come on, come on. There was no meconium staining. He just needed to breathe. Breathe, and he'd be okay.

Piper exclaimed, "What do I do?"

"Breathe, baby," Ella said sternly. Again, she clamped two fingers around the umbilical cord and swept down the cord toward the baby. "Come on. You're in the air. You can do it."

She bagged him again. "Breathe. Two. Three. Breathe. Two. Three. Piper." Piper started. "Put your hand on his chest. Gentle circles."

Adam said, "Three minutes."

She kept up the rhythm. *Breathe. Two. Three.* The baby's chest was rising and falling, but not without her help. Was his skin pinking up?

She checked his heartbeat.

Ninety. "Keep it up," she ordered, then bagged the baby again. *Breathe. Two. Three.* But now his chest was rising and falling better, and yes, his skin was definitely pinker than before.

She pulled off the bag to get another heartbeat, and the baby startled, gasped, then let out a wail.

Piper cried out, and she threw herself over her child. Blinking hard, Ella rushed to wrap him back in the warm blankets. He shrieked again, and she laid him in his mother's arms.

He was breathing. Breath in. Breath out. Over and over, he was doing it on his own.

Piper's face was streaked with tears. "Is he okay? Is he going to be okay?"

"Yes." Ella swallowed, battling tears of her own. "You thought the heartbeat was the best sound in the world, but when he screamed? That was the best."

Chapter Twenty-One

For all that Ella said the baby was going to be okay, she wasn't acting like it.

Adam had never in his life seen anything like what she'd done, that moment she'd transformed from, "Oh, sweetie, you're doing great," to "Piper—hands and knees, *now!*" and then seized control of every little detail. Putting that mask on the baby's face while he was still half-inside Piper? Putting her fingers up inside trying to grab the baby's armpit?

Then the way she'd kept her calm the whole time everything was going off the rails?

When had Adam ever seen someone do that? Instead of panicking, Ella had taken command—first of herself, then over the rest of the situation. She'd assessed, chosen a course of action, followed it, and not given up. His grandson was alive because of her. If Piper had given birth alone the way Kandace had, that baby would be dead. Piper might even be dead.

Then instead of congratulating herself, Ella had kept right on working. She "bagged the baby" again over and over for the next hour, putting that mask back on him to assist his breathing, keeping him as warm as she could in a house without heat.

They'd used thermal packs and blankets to wrap the baby skin to skin with Piper, and they kept heating new blankets over at the woodstove to wrap them up together. Eventually Piper moved right up beside it, and Adam had returned from the kitchen with a sports drink for her only to find Ella cleaning the birthing area.

Piper was sitting there with her baby, cuddling him and staring at him in the dark. Adam looked once over her shoulder, and the baby had his eyes wide open, looking right back at her.

After all that baby had been through, he wasn't even crying. Once he'd settled down, he just wanted to be held, wanted to observe. Quiet and alert, he introduced himself to his new world, but he did it by studying his mother.

Oh, and the placenta. Piper had delivered the placenta, and then Ella had examined it in a bowl, shining her flashlight over the whole thing. "Do you want to see it?" she'd asked Piper. "With all the blood vessels, it looks like a tree," and Piper had breathed an awed yes. Adam had excused himself to find something to take care of in the kitchen. Anything.

"I don't need to experience all of it," he told Moonie, who'd followed him there.

The living room lightened as the sun rose. Ella showed Piper how to offer her breast to the baby, and the baby latched on. Piper exclaimed, "Hey! Ow," and Ella said, "Good. That's what's called an afterpain, and it means you're recovering."

So many details. "Delivering a baby" should have meant putting on gloves and catching, not examining the mess left behind after delivery and estimating that Piper had lost six hundred milliliters of blood.

Ella came into the kitchen to wash her hands again. "You might as well get some rest. I'm going to stay all morning to monitor her and the baby."

Adam said, "You did great."

Ella looked aside. "Piper did great. She labored really well, kept her cool, and did everything she needed to."

Adam said, "I know that. What I said was, you did great."

As she shut the water, he put his hand on her. "I'm really sorry how I went off on you about the crib."

"You were right that I was overstepping." Ella turned to him. "I have no say over what Piper does with her life. I forgot my role was to stay with her while she steered the course."

Adam said, "But you were doing your job, and I let my ego get in the way. You told me the crib wasn't to code, and I heard you saying I was a lousy father. I'm sorry about that."

She met his eyes in the dim kitchen. He opened his arms, and she stepped into his hug.

"Can you give me another chance?" she asked.

"Can you forgive me?"

In response, she raised her face to his, and they kissed, long and slow.

Around them, the lights flared on.

"Hey!" Ella laughed. "Look what you did."

"What I did?" Adam shook his head. "Pretty sure you're the one caused the power surge."

He kissed her again, just to see if that would do anything else. In the basement, the heater roared to life. He pulled away just enough to murmur, "I'm liking this magic."

Piper called, "Hey, guys? Check this out."

Pink-cheeked, Ella went into the living room. Piper nodded toward the baby in her arms. "He latched on again! I thought he was asleep, but I guess he turned his face and it was a reflex or something."

"He's doing great." Ella looked around. "Once it warms up more, we'll heat up some water and clean the both of you up a bit. When he wakes up, we're going to do the newborn assessment examination, and we can tell you what your little chunk weighs. I'm guessing seven and a half pounds. And you," she said, turning back to Adam.

Miming disbelief, Adam gestured to himself.

"Yes, you. You're going to need to get some sleep because you were up all night, too."

Adam folded his arms. "Not until I get what I want. I want to know the baby's name."

Piper said, "Really? You're holding your own sleep hostage until I tell you?"

"Yes. I refuse to lie down and close my eyes until I know what I'm going to be calling my own grandson."

Piper gazed back at the baby tucked under the blanket with her.

Ella said, "Are you going with Maverick?"

Piper looked up. "You know… Everything you said last night…?" Her lip quivered. "You're right about everything. Dad, I'm sorry I didn't trust you. You've always been there for me, and you never asked for anything. Grayson wanted to name the baby Skylar, and I do, too."

"Skylar." Adam crouched down to stroke the baby's forehead with all that dark hair. "I like it. You tell Grayson he picked a good name. And a good mom for his baby."

"Dad!" Piper rolled her eyes. "Get me my phone. Now that we've got light and internet, I should send Grayson some pictures. Oh, and post everywhere. Everyone's going to want to know."

Adam took pictures with Piper's phone and then with his. Then Ella used both their phones and took pictures with him and her and the baby.

Adam waved her over. "One more. You get in it."

When Ella shook her head, he said, "No, I want you in here. Piper's started a family today, and if we're taking family photos, then I want you in some, too."

EPILOGUE

Ella shrieked as Adam steered the snowmobile over another hill, then picked up speed on the downhill. She leaned forward, glad he was taking the brunt of the wind and even more glad for the goggles and heated gloves.

They took the track into the woods, and he slowed a bit as the trees whipped by.

This was fantastic. He'd warned her to keep her hands "inside" the snowmobile, but even on a snowmobile designed for two people, she was way too scared to let go of the handgrips. He'd also issued a stern warning about not standing on the sled, but come on. She had her feet planted on the running boards and wouldn't have moved them for a thousand dollars.

The snow was fun, but she'd rather be riding on it than tumbling into it.

The lodge came into view, and Ella felt simultaneous relief and disappointment. This was a lot of fun, but also, this was a lot of cold. She was ready to be done with it for a little while.

Adam parked the snowmobile, and he got down first before helping her off. "Thanks." She rubbed her hands together to restore circulation. "That was wild!"

"See, I knew you'd like it!" Adam's cheeks were windblown, and he looked ecstatic. "Let's get warmed up a bit before we go back out."

Inside the lodge, Ella didn't dare to unzip her coat. Adam planted her on a couch near a tremendous fireplace, and then he returned with hot apple cider. "Here, this will do you."

"Thanks." She forced herself to take off her gloves and immediately wrapped her hands around the cup. "That was definitely better than doing the same thing in the dark during a blizzard."

Settling beside her, Adam put an arm over her shoulder, and she rested her head on him.

The lodge with its open woodwork had a rustic feel, and in every direction, they had views of snow-covered mountains. Mid-week, not many skiers used the lodge, so it wasn't too noisy. They also couldn't stay very late. They'd come just for the day because it was Ella's day off, and Adam had been able to schedule around her.

After sensation returned to her toes, Ella got brave enough to unzip her jacket. She watched the fire, aware that time was ticking away. They ought to try another trail, but Adam felt so comfortable beside her.

Adam sounded hesitant. "I've been thinking about where to go from here."

They'd started with the simplest snowmobile track. She hoped he wouldn't aim straight for the most difficult one next.

He added, his voice rich and deep, "With Skylar's first birthday and then Piper's wedding coming up and everything, I know it's a lot."

Oh. Not that kind of "where to go from here." Ella said, "What will you do after she moves out?"

"It's going to be pretty quiet all of a sudden." Adam shifted so she would sit up, and when she faced him, he looked serious. "You and I both came out of bad situations, but I keep feeling like there was a meaning to the way we worked our way to each other. Piper was in a bad spot, and you helped her, and I helped her, and somehow in all that helping, you and I found each other."

He took Ella's small hand in his warm ones. "What I'm saying is, we started the right way, by working together to help Piper start a family, but I think we may also have ended up on the way to starting our own family. I love you, Ella. I love you, and I want to have a family of our own. Will you marry me?"

Ella laid her other hand on his. "I love you too, and yes, I will marry you."

Adam kissed her, then pulled a ring box from an inner pocket of his jacket. He flipped the top to reveal an emerald on a slender band of white gold. He removed it from the velvet compartment and slipped it onto her finger, and then Ella kissed him again.

They had the rest of the day before them, trails to ride, news to tell Piper, dinner, and the long ride home again. But for now, Ella wrapped her arms around Adam, her cheek against his flannel shirt, and closed her eyes. The future was right here. The future was open before them both.

THANK YOU!

Thank you so much for reading about Adam and Ella! This was a fun story to write, and I ended up Googling all sorts of wild things, from "how to strip an umbilical cord" to "how much does a snowmobile weigh?"

I'd like to thank my early readers and my plot-stormers. Also thank you to Virginia McKevitt for her cover, Marie Higgins for organizing the series, and Judy O'Gara for editing.

I've written a bunch of other stories about Hartwell, Maine, as well as the neighboring town of Brighthead. If you're interested, please check out those romances over at Amazon.

Also, please-please-please consider leaving a review for this book over at Goodreads or Amazon. It doesn't have to be a book report—just a star rating and a couple of lines about what you liked or didn't like. I'd really appreciate it, and reviews help both authors and other readers.

I keep a mailing list at http://eepurl.com/dEJjI1 where you can enjoy "Maddie Mondays." Most Mondays, I'll send an email with a brief anecdote about my weird life plus a recommendation for something you might enjoy—a book, a knitting pattern, a recipe...? It's kind of fun, and I'd love to see you there.

Thank you again so much for spending time in Hartwell, and until next time, keep reading!

READ ABOUT MORE HEALTH CARE HEROES!

If you enjoyed this story, please check out the other novellas about our healthcare heroes! They're all available (or will be available) for Amazon Kindle and Kindle Unlimited.